TWISTED DECEPTION

A NOVEL

LETICIA TWYMAN

Twisted Deception

This novel is a work of fiction. Any references to real people, events, establishments or locales are intended only to give the fiction a sense of reality and authenticity. Other names, characters, and incidents occurring in the work either are the product of the author's imagination or are used fictitiously, as are those fictionalized events and incidents that involve real persons. Any character that happens to share the name of a person who is or has been an acquaintance to the author is purely coincidental and is in no way intended to be an actual account involving that person.

EBook ISBN 978-0-9974033-0-5
Paperback ISBN 978-0-9974033-1-2

Cover layout and graphic design by: Leticia Twyman
Typesetting: Leticia Twyman and Amelda Stukes
Editor: Amelda Stukes and FirstEditing.com

Twisted Deception: A novel by Leticia Twyman
Leticia.twyman@yahoo.com

Dedication

"I Love You."

"Still?"

"Always."

ACKNOWLEDGMENTS

This project would not have been possible without the support I received from so many people on so many levels. But first of all, I have to thank my Lord and Savior, Jesus Christ, for my imaginative gift and the ability to relay it on paper. I could never take your power over my life for granted! Lord, you are awesome! Thank you Aunt Shirley Seegars for helping to guide my spiritual path. I truly appreciate your time and wisdom.

I thank my family, Michael T., Tytianna B., Jasmine T., and Myka T., as well as my grandbabies, Benton W., Deyanah B., Ah'Zaria W. and Delilah B., for always believing, supporting and listening to my visions while giving me the time and space I needed work. I love you all!

Nothing would be possible without my mothers, Betty P. Barnes and Dorothy R. Holley. Yes, I'm blessed to have two! Betty P. Barnes ensured that I could read and write at an early age, made me read and write daily, taught me more than any teacher could and taught me the value of education. She instilled the discipline I needed to make it in this world. I wouldn't be able to do any of this without the early guidance she gave me. The foundation she gave me was phenomenal. I love you!

My other mother, Dorothy Ray Holley, a retired science teacher of 32 years, also helped mold me into the woman I am by teaching me and giving me the unconditional love and support I needed to believe in my abilities to make this vision come to fruition. She encouraged me to pursue my gift of writing and was one of the first to tell me over 15 years ago that I should write a book! The love I have for her can't be defined!

My good friend and supporter Curtis Rock, a Christian Hip/Hop artist, for listening to me, giving me spiritual guidance and vision, supporting my dream and pushing me forward when I would lose my focus. Thank you so much! I wish the best for you in all your endeavors as well.

There are so many more people to acknowledge from the DC Public school system in general (Fletcher Johnson back in the 80s, Mrs. Campbell/English and Mr. Muhammed/Science, Ms. Dobbins/Algebra and Dr. Rutherford our principal--even Coach Moe). I love you all for helping to educate me! I attended college but I do not have any notable accolades there. No offense, but I don't.

Thank you to all my best girlfriends/Aces, LaBresha Butler, owner of Pino's Playground and a sister-friend for over 30 years; Patricia Lee, sister-friend for 27 years; Sabrina H., so positive and an excellent supporter, as well as Christa Matthews, who is also an excellent poet. Christa was another positive motivating force in my life who pushed me to finish my goal. I'm going to push her to publish her poems in the near future.

Mr. E. Osborn! Oh yeah! I will never forget the day that I was reading passages from the book to him. He thought it was a book I had purchased from Kindle. He kept asking me for the name of the book because he thought his wife would like to read it. I kept blowing him off by telling him that I didn't want to scroll to the beginning of the book to find out (laughing to myself). Anyway, I finally asked him what he thought the book should be called. He still had no idea I was the author. He didn't hesitate when he exclaimed, "Twisted!" He said, "Every time you think one thing is going to happen, something else happens. Everything is just twisted!" It was the best blind test of a product ever! I revealed that I was the author. He was amazed and the genuinely shocked look on his face will be embedded in my brain forever. He made me read pages to him all day and told me if I stopped, he would treat me like the movie "Misery!" His idea ultimately gave birth to my title, *Twisted Deception.* It was an awesome day and awesome revelation to finally have a title for my book! Love you, Ozzy! I thank you dearly!

Last but not least, a huge shout out to my ACE, Yin-Yang twin, supporter and confidante, Amelda Stukes, AKA Mel Mel, who helped initially edit and guide me for this debut novel. She kept it on track all the way. She has been more than a best friend for over 30 years. She has been the sister I never had! I love you!

Ok, enough of that mushy stuff--let's get to the book! I hope you enjoy every page.

Email your ideas, comments and suggestions anytime to:
leticia.twyman@yahoo.com

PROLOGUE

Dwight got into his sleek black Mercedes and headed to the interstate to meet Joy. The traffic was heavy and he wished he had left much sooner. It took over four hours to make a three hour drive, but he was happy he made it. There were always limited parking spaces available in Joy's community late at night so he had to park his black Benz a few blocks from the condominiums. Dwight had stopped at a twenty-four hour grocery store to pick up some flowers for Joy. He reached into the backseat and retrieved the flowers and a card.

As he walked down the street, he rehearsed what he was going to say to Joy when he saw her beautiful face. Suddenly, he caught a glimpse of a shadowy figure a few feet behind him. The person startled him slightly and he jumped from the discovery as he thought, *Where did they come from?* He turned around to try to take a better look at the person but couldn't see past the bright lamppost that was shining directly into his eyes. Dwight laughed as he regained his composure and continued down the sidewalk. He turned the corner, still a few blocks away from the condo, and heard three gunshots. He began to fall forward and landed face-down on the concrete. He gasped for air and felt a terrible burning sensation that went into his back and through the mid-section of his chest. He could see the beautiful yellow and red mixed roses strewn across the pavement, spattered with blood. He knew now that he had been shot and that the blood he saw was his. As he looked at the flowers, a tear fell from his eye and he thought, *Not like this, not now--what about Joy and my baby?* He couldn't move. He felt the blood seeping from his body to the ground and he could see a glimmer of red from the reflection it gave off the light shining from the lamppost. His body became cold and he began to shake. Suddenly, he tasted metal on his tongue and saw darkness approaching until there wasn't any light left to see.

Chapter 1 - Change of Venue

"I THINK WE'RE LOST. Maybe we should have waited until later in the morning to leave," John stated to Joy, who was sitting in the front passenger seat of the rented Tahoe truck.

"Maybe, but I need to get everything set up as soon as possible. My classes will be starting soon and I have to find childcare for Sonya and get Sophie registered for school. But honestly, with everything that was happening to me, I couldn't wait another minute to get away from that place. I don't understand it, but everything just seemed to go wrong for me there. Maybe I was just jinxed or something. I don't know," Joy said.

"I doubt that very much. Things will be different for you now you'll see," John stated confidently as he looked toward Joy and gently patted her thigh.

"You have always been so supportive. Thank you, John. I don't know where we would be without all your help. You have truly been the one blessing in my life."

Joy looked in the backseat toward her daughters, who were both sleeping. Sophie, age eight, was holding onto her favorite doll and Sonya, nine months, was in her car-seat with her pacifier still in her mouth. Joy turned back around and smiled at the decision she made to relocate to another city with her daughters.

John glanced over at Joy and asked, "What are you over there smiling about?"

Joy looked deeply into John's eyes and replied, "Everything."

John returned the smile then looked back toward the street. He was happy that after all this time Joy seemed just as interested in him as he was in her. They continued to drive in silence on the highway, both consumed in their own private thoughts.

"We made it, little ones," John said as he opened the door for Sophie to get out of the backseat of the truck.

Sophie looked around but didn't see anything remotely familiar. "Where are we?" she asked John.

Joy got out of the truck and answered, "We are at our new home."

Sophie looked around the low-scale apartment complex her mother called their new home. There was trash all over the ground, a vacant lot filled with abandoned cars and a corner store full of people just standing around beside the complex.

"Can you watch Sonya for me, John, while I go get the keys?" asked Joy.

"I'm mad you felt you had to ask me that," John said jokingly. "No Joy, I will not stay here and watch Sonya. Not even for a million dollars."

Joy laughed at John's comment, then she retrieved her purse from the truck and closed the door. Sophie grabbed her mother's hand as they walked into the rental office. "Hello, I'm Joy, Joy Masterson. I'm here to pick up the keys to my apartment," she stated to the man at the counter. The man hung up the telephone and just smiled. Joy stared briefly at the young man. He wore an expensive-looking yellow shirt and tie and a professionally tailored blazer. His eyebrows were trimmed perfectly and it appeared that he wore a slight pinkish shade of lip-gloss to accentuate his lips. He was completely clean-cut and professional as he stated, "Hello ma'am. I'm Peter. I'm sorry, how may I help you again?"

"I just arrived in town and would like to pick up my keys to my apartment," Joy explained again.

The man placed his perfectly manicured hands on the worn counter and stated, "I'm sorry, ma'am, there must be some misunderstanding. We do not have anyone scheduled to move into our residence for over three months. We don't even have any vacancies at this time."

"Excuse me? This must be a mistake. I paid my security deposit already and I have a lease agreement that I received over a month ago. Let me show it to you." Joy began to look in her purse for her paperwork but couldn't locate it anywhere.

"Ma'am, I'm so sorry for the confusion. The manager will be in next week if you would like to give her a call. There's nothing I can do for you." Joy could have sworn she heard Peter pop his lips after making his last statement.

"Look sir, aren't you even gonna try to check? I just moved from out of town with my daughters. Everything I own is out there in that trailer that's attached to that truck, and I don't have anywhere else to go. Can you reach the manager and find out what is going on? This is ridiculous!"

"I would love to but she is actually out of the country on vacation. I can suggest a few really nice hotels in the vicinity you could choose from until she returns. I'm sure she will be able to sort this whole thing out."

John walked in the rental office, holding Sonya. Sophie ran to him and said, "They don't have a place for us to stay." Joy shook her head and walked back to the truck with Sophie in search of her rental agreement.

John walked up to the counter where the man stood and asked, "Hello, are you Peter?"

"Yes. Yes, I am." John immediately recognized the femininity in the man's voice that confirmed it was the same person he had talked to over the phone just seconds ago as well as the past few weeks.

"So here is the money I owe you, as promised." John handed Peter a brown envelope.

Peter tilted his head to the side then smiled and said, "Wow, this was the easiest and largest commission I've ever made in my whole life. Do you want to know what I told her?"

"No. That won't be necessary. But this remains between us, understand?" John stared directly at Peter for a response.

Peter opened the envelope below the counter just in case Joy returned. He counted the balance of the money John gave him to keep Joy out of the apartment at all costs, then he responded, "Looks like we have an agreement to me, Mr. Moneybags. Who are you again? You must really love this broad." Peter laughed at his own joke as John remained stone-faced, glaring at Peter.

Peter took note of John's reaction and stated, "My bad, I just figured you must be into this chick to break me off with five thousand dollars."

John looked sternly at Peter and said, "That's none of your business."

Both men ceased talking when the bell on the rental office door jingled. Joy and Sophie reentered the office and Joy looked even more frustrated than before. "I can't find those papers anywhere! I know I had them. That was the first thing I put in my bag! What am I going to do now?" John walked over to Joy, then reached out and touched both of her shoulders. "Let me go find a nice room for the night. Then we can sort all this out another day."

"John, I can't afford to just be getting rooms all over the place." Joy swung her arms in the air in frustration. "I paid for this place and I don't understand why I can't get my keys and move in like I was told over the phone." Joy was starting to raise her voice and glared at Peter behind the counter who seemed like he could care less about her situation.

"There is nothing that young man can do. If he could, he would have already. Let's just go find a room nearby. You know I'll take care of it for you and you wouldn't owe me a thing." John smiled encouragingly at Joy.

"Well, I guess I don't have much of a choice right now, do I, John?" John ushered Joy and Sophie out of the rental office as he looked back at Peter and winked his eye. Peter winked back as John shut the door behind them.

Joy, Sophie, and Sonya sat quietly in the truck while John drove away from the run-down apartment complex to a really nice hotel located about twenty minutes away. John looked over at Joy and said, "Don't worry. Everything will be okay. You stress too much." John jumped out of the truck and headed into the office to book a room. In less than five minutes, John walked back out of the hotel to the truck.

"So they didn't have any availability, huh?" Joy asked.

"Yes, why would you think that? Here are your keys right here," said John. Joy looked at John in amazement and tried to figure out how he was able to book a room so quickly.

"They must have excellent customer service for you to book a room that fast!" Joy said inquisitively.

John just smiled as he thought, *Yes, they do because it was already booked and waiting on me, my dear.* But John didn't respond; instead, he parked the big truck and trailer in the back of the hotel lot and removed their luggage for the evening. "Come on, my ladies. Let's go see the room."

Sophie eagerly jumped out of the truck. She thought this place looked much better than the last one. It had an indoor pool and recreation room as well as a pancake house right across the street from the hotel. They took the elevator to the ninth floor and entered a beautifully decorated suite that included a mini kitchenette. Joy looked around and wondered how she was going to afford such a place, but was thankful that she allowed John to help her make this major move after all.

"So how do you like it, Joy? Will this be okay for at least a week or so?" John asked.

"Nawwww, I'd rather all of us sleep in the truck. Of course, it's okay. I just don't know how I will ever pay you back for all this."

"Well, for now how about you let me sleep on the sleep sofa for the night." John smiled.

"Of course, you can stay as long as you like." Joy joked around like it was truly her apartment. The room was gorgeous. It was nothing like the apartment she was about to rent for the year. The room was decorated in expensive pieces of artwork and furnishings throughout. The kitchenette's counter was made of granite and the faucets were a gold and silver blend. Nothing about this place was inexpensive. Joy knew John had money but never knew how much. But at this point, she was beginning to wonder.

The hotel room door opened and John began to exit. "Joy, I'll be back in a little while. You and the kids can get settled in. I need to pick up a few things and handle some business calls. See you in a few hours, okay?" John didn't give Joy a chance to respond before he walked out the door.

Chapter 2 - Cause of Disturbance

JOHN DISCONNECTED the trailer from the tow hitch of the truck, jumped in and pulled out of the parking space at the Appalachian Suites. He headed to the closest grocery store so he could fully stock the little kitchen with food for his new ready-made family.

He had already reserved the room a week in advance since his true surprise wouldn't be ready for another week. He smiled as he thought that the deal with Peter went perfectly. Joy didn't have any idea what was going on, and that was his intention. He knew Joy was smart and wished he had thought to stall before returning to the truck so fast with the keys to the room. But he figured he had played it off pretty well. After everything he had been through to get close to Joy these last two years, there was no way he was going to let her move away and not know how to locate her. They had gotten really close after Sonya's birth, and John wanted to get even closer.

He admired how Joy always tried to be independent but he knew she wasn't prepared for this major move. And unbeknownst to her, the only reason she was moving was because of him in the first place. So he had to make sure he was in the vicinity to bail her out when she needed it. She would refuse any help he tried to provide for her, so he had to always make it appear like she had no other choice. After what occurred, he had established that Joy and her children were his responsibility. He knew her life would be so much different if it wasn't for his fatal attraction to her. He also knew if she ever found out the truth about him or that he was behind all the misfortune she had to endure, she would hate him and probably refuse to ever see him again. The guilt that built up inside him daily was insurmountable. But he was determined to fix it. His goal was to make her fall in love with him so that when she learned the truth she would forgive him and they could move on and have a happy life together. At this point, he knew she was at least interested but he wanted to find the perfect time to permanently transition their long friendship into a full relationship.

John arrived at the grocery store. He spoke to the cashier, who gave him a flirtatious smile as he passed by. But he had no interest in anyone besides Joy. John constantly asked himself why he couldn't just play it off and act like he was happy. He was married with a company worth millions of dollars. He owned a fifteen thousand square foot home that spanned over one hundred acres of property. His bank account would make any woman happy but even with all of that he still wasn't happy. He wanted out of his situation and he still had no idea how he was even going to make Joy aware of any of it. She knew he had a company but had no idea how large it really was. She only knew of his small apartment in Juniper. He felt he should have told her the truth about his life a long time ago, but he couldn't for fear she wouldn't want anything to do with him. Now, he felt he had no choice but to keep Joy and her girls safe.

John's cell phone began to ring. It rang several times during the trip but he had the ringer on silent. He knew exactly who it was and he had no intention of talking to her. John shook his head, trying to erase the thought of his wife from his mind and started back shopping. He looked down at the expensive timepiece on his wrist. He had finished the grocery shopping but figured neither he nor Joy would feel like cooking after taking that long drive. So he picked up three dinners from the pancake house across the street from the hotel and headed back to the hotel.

John knocked at the hotel room door. He could hear Sonya crying and then the pitter patter of Sophie's feet running to the door. "Who is it?" Sophie asked with her innocent little voice.

"It's me." John answered.

Sophie quickly unlocked the door. "Hiiii, Mr. John!" John smiled at Sophie as he carried several bags to the kitchenette.

Joy walked out of the bedroom and into the small living room area holding Sonya. "Sophie! What did I tell you about opening the door without telling me?!"

"It's my fault, Joy," John interjected. "I told her it was me. Don't be too hard on her this time."

"She has to stop that, John. It's not safe. She has to learn not to just open doors for people until she asks me! No matter who it is!"

"Ok, ok, you are right. Did you hear that, sweetie?" John looked towards Sophie and said, "Don't open doors without telling your mom first from now on, okay?"

"Even if it's you, Mr. John?"

"Yes. Even if it's me. Now let's eat."

Joy shook her head and headed back into the bedroom to lay Sonya down. John noticed Joy had changed her clothes into something more comfortable and thought how beautiful she was even without makeup. He wished he could walk up to her and plant his lips in every place imaginable on her. But he knew he couldn't. If she walked up and embraced him, he would be happy. But instead of her walking up to him to embrace him, she simply asked, "Hey John, I thought you had a key to the room? Why did you knock in the first place?"

"Yes, I have a key. But I figured my ladies might want a little privacy. I can't just bust in the room like that, now can I? Soooo, are my ladies a little hungry? You all should be by now."

Joy smiled and said, "Your ladies? You like to call us that, huh? I don't know if I like it; it sounds a little creepish. Creepish," Joy repeated the word then laughed to herself. "Is that even a word? Hmmm, well, I can say that you are the best friend ever, *With your fine ass self,* she thought. *So I won't knock it at all.*

"Well to answer your question, dear, creepish is not a word," John said and they both laughed.

Joy and Sophie sat down at the little bar area adjacent to the miniature kitchen to eat as John sipped his soda in front of the television, watching the evening news. John began to drift away into his own thoughts of Joy. Being in this environment with her and the children made him feel like they were his own personal little family.

John first encountered Joy at church. He would watch her from afar every time she visited but he never approached her. Then she stopped coming to the church altogether and for months he hadn't seen her. One night, during a business dinner at a local restaurant and lounge, John spotted Joy seated at the bar with friends. He was completely intrigued by her entire persona. She seemed to be quiet and even a little shy. She was wearing a pair of black fitted jeans with a black pullover top embellished with silver sequins around the neckline. Her hair was curled tight in the front with a few tendrils that flowed around the sides of her mocha-colored skin, accentuating her high cheekbones. The back of her hair was pinned up into a high bun and John imagined what it would look like if it were unpinned. She wore a little bit of eyeliner with no foundation, unlike a lot of the other women he saw in the lounge. Her low-heeled pumps matched her small silver clutch bag which she sat on the bar in front of her. She had a humbleness about her that personified her existence. In her simple black jeans and blouse, she glowed beyond the many women who wore fancy, expensive clothing and teeny-tiny, tight mini-dresses for attention.

The entire time John watched her, she never ordered an alcoholic beverage. He noticed that the bartender brought her several orange sodas during her stay as she laughed and conversed with her friends. He watched her throughout his entire business meeting and she never even noticed him. As the evening came to an end, John finalized his meeting and walked his newest contractor to the door as he welcomed him to the company. He returned to continue to watch Joy but never approached her or tried to speak to her. He just continued to watch her all night from across the room. Joy never left her barstool except to go to the restroom. She didn't strut around looking for attention and she didn't get inebriated like some of her girlfriends. John fell in love with what he saw of her that same day. The day she never knew he existed.

John left the restaurant but could not shake the thought of wanting to meet Joy on a personal level. He wished he had approached her that evening to at least try. He didn't know anything about her besides the couple he saw her accompany from time to time at church. So one day he approached the man, who turned out to be her brother

Patrick, and asked him about the mysterious woman who had accompanied him and his wife Susan to the church. John got straight to the point and asked if she would be joining the church anytime soon. John was a respected businessman in the town, and although Patrick didn't really know John, he knew he was someone of some importance around town. So Patrick welcomed the inquiry and even added more information than what was requested. By the time they finished talking, John had learned that Joy was Patrick's younger sister, recently divorced, living with them and working at the local pharmacy in Sheppard's Market as a pharmacy technician. He also knew which college she was currently attending and even that she was majoring in pharmacy with the intention of becoming a doctor of pharmacy.

John wasn't surprised at how forthright her brother and sister-in-law were with their information. He was used to people giving him what he wanted, simply because of his wife's family's name. All he had to do was mention the fact that he was affiliated with the Conglins and his wish would be granted. John just used the excuse of needing more good people to join the congregation at the church and went on his way. Patrick and Susan smiled, feeling honored to speak with John, and left. Never once did they suspect he was just trying to get information to locate Joy. In reality, John couldn't care less about the church or the congregation. He barely attended church and had only started attending on a regular basis to see if he could possibly run into Joy again. And it worked, because he got exactly what he wanted and more.

After learning Joy worked at the pharmacy, John knew he had to find a way to run into her naturally. So he made a doctor's appointment and complained of not being able to sleep at night. His doctor prescribed him a sleep aid and he took the prescription to the Sheppard's Market to see if he could run into her there. He visited the pharmacy three times before he finally saw Joy working. John had already planned how he would try to get her into his life. What to do about his current wife and her family was another story.

***

Joy thought of how she should be married and comfortable, living in a nice home with a picket fence and maybe even more little ones running around. But that wasn't the case at all. Instead she was a divorced single parent, who recently got pregnant and was abandoned with another man's child, career-less, back in college like a young adult and living with her brother for the past two years. What a contrast. Joy stood in the bathroom and glared at her beautiful reflection in the mirror. Joy was 5'8 and 155 pounds with a cinnamon complexion. She had shoulder-length dark brown hair that she commonly wore in tight curls in the front and pinned up in the back. She had a natural beauty and a firecracker personality. But she never recognized her own beauty and thought of herself as mediocre.

How did my life end up like this? Joy asked herself as she banged her fist on the marbled bathroom counter.

Joy walked into the kitchen and poured a glass of Orange Crush soda John had picked up from the grocery store. *He knows me so well,* she thought as she sipped her favorite drink then headed to the terrace that overlooked the pool area. As Joy plopped herself down on the plush lounge chair, she thought of how she had to move in with her older brother Patrick and his wife Susan in a small town called Juniper after divorcing her abusive husband, Timothy. Then she thought of Dwight, the man she fell in love with and unexpectedly became pregnant by. Joy looked over her shoulder and through the patio glass door at Sonya, nestled peacefully in John's arms as if she were his child.

How could your father not accept you? How could he never come back to check on us, not even once? she thought.

Joy felt herself about to cry and turned around to gaze off the terrace view once more. Sophie looked toward her mother sitting alone on the terrace then headed to the patio door. She pushed the heavy door open and stuck her little head out.

"You okay, Mommy?" Sophie so innocently asked.

"Yes, baby girl. Everything is okay." Sophie looked over the terrace to the pool then ran back inside with John, obviously to inquire about the pool.

Joy watched as her daughter eagerly ran to a man who was simply her friend and wondered why he didn't have a family of his own. John practically helped raise Sophie and Sonya from behind the scenes. Joy turned back around and thought of how blessed she was to have someone helping her with no strings attached, but after this past year she looked at John differently. She now wanted more and didn't know how to let him know since they had been only friends for so long. She began to silently pray that her new life away from Juniper would be much better for them. She silently vowed to God she would to do whatever she could to make their lives better.

Chapter 3 - Before the Move

JOY WORKED long hours as much as she could throughout the first six months of her pregnancy with Sonya. She attended college classes and set a number of goals for her life. She wished she had completed her classes years ago but her ex-husband Timothy was a complete control freak and didn't want her to do anything besides sit home. After their divorce and Joy's move to Juniper, everything seemed okay. Timothy would see Sophie on occasion and their relationship was actually civil.

However, after her second pregnancy everything in Joy's life went extremely wrong overnight. It started one day when she reported to work and the general manager told her that her position had been discontinued due to the company's new budgeting restrictions. She had worked at the pharmacy at Sheppard's Market for months and didn't understand why her position was the only position being discontinued. But she figured it wouldn't be difficult to find another job, so she applied for all types of positions at any and all types of locations with no luck. No matter how much she tried, she couldn't find employment anywhere. No one seemed to be willing to hire her. Joy was visibly pregnant at this point so she figured they just didn't want to invest in a temporary employee, because she knew she was more than qualified for the positions for which she applied.

Her brother told her not to stress and that she and her children could stay with them as long as she wanted. He owned a nice three-bedroom condominium with two full baths and plenty of space. Patrick and Susan owned several wedding boutiques in the area. They were more than capable of supporting Joy, Sophie, and the new baby. But Joy didn’t feel comfortable with her brother and sister-in-law taking care of her and her children. She desperately felt the need to contribute to the household in some way, so she resorted to going to the local social services office to get WIC and food stamps. However, shortly after she began receiving food stamps, they were stopped due to fraud allegations. Between losing her job and losing her assistance, Joy didn't know what was going on. Her pregnancy was the last thing she expected, especially since she was on birth control the whole time she was involved with Dwight. Now she wished she hadn't gotten careless and aroused to the point of not using a condom on a few occasions. She remembered the night she must have conceived. She and Dwight got it on hot and heavy right on her brother’s bathroom floor. Joy thought briefly of having an abortion but quickly dismissed the thought. Joy was raised to take care of her responsibilities and if God felt it was time for her to have a child then who was she to deny it?

Joy looked up into the sky. The sun was setting and the sight of it all was beautiful.

I should have moved away from Juniper years ago. Time goes by so fast. I just wasted the last few years of my life going in circles with school, random jobs and men. Yes, this is the right decision, to move away and get a fresh start. I need to leave everything behind, including John, even though he has been the one positive thing in my life. However, I doubt if he wants to make me and the children a full time responsibility. For some reason he reminds me so much of Dwight. I pray that's not why Dwight abandoned me. He swore that John and I had something going on besides just a friendship. And although I have feelings for John now, Dwight was completely wrong back then. What if Dwight thinks this is John's baby? What if.... Joy shifted her weight in the chair again. *I just need to restart my life and get a fresh new start.* Joy shook away her thoughts as she stood up and went back into the hotel room from the terrace to be with John and her children.

Later that evening, John, Joy, Sophie and Sonya sat in the living room watching cable like the perfect, happy little family until Joy broke the silence to say, "Hey John, I think Sophie, Sonya and I can go ahead over to Charlene's tomorrow."

John looked at Joy in surprise. "Who is Charlene?"

"My cousin. We have always been pretty close. I haven't seen her in a while but I'm sure she wouldn't mind if we stayed with her for a while."

John thought, *Damn, I didn't factor in that she might already have a backup plan.*

"What do you mean? I booked this suite for you and the girls for the entire week!" John exclaimed.

"I understand that, John. I just don't feel comfortable staying here like this and not paying anything, because nothing in life is free. Just cancel the room for the rest of the week and I'll pay you for the day we used."

"Joy, I am not going to let you pay me a dime. But I really wish you would just stay here at least for the rest of the week. The bill is already taken care of. No strings attached," John pleaded.

Joy looked over at Sophie and Sonya, who were now fast asleep on the couch. John had taken Sophie to the pool for a little while and she was exhausted. Joy thought, *John is really doing too much for us. He needs to go home. He's just making my feelings stronger for him.* Joy looked over at John, who was still patiently waiting for a response.

"John, I just don't know. You have to go back to work and I have to get on with my life. I don't even understand why you do most of the stuff you do for us." Joy fiddled with her hands and looked down at her feet, hoping he would reveal that he wanted more. "You have been by my side for almost two years now and believe me, John, I'm quite thankful. I just don't feel I deserve to be treated this way."

"I'm here to tell you and show you that you are. It has been easy to see that you're not used to a man taking care of you without asking for something in return. Or maybe it's just that you're extra-determined and strong-willed, but either way, I don't have a problem with helping you and your children right now. That's what real friends are for, Joy." Then John thought, *Did I just use the friend word?* and quickly regretted it. "Let me help you and the children until you get on your feet. Everything will be okay, I promise."

Joy turned back to John, who appeared to be deep in thought now. "Ok, we will stay but just for this week."

John looked up and smiled. "Ok. That's great. That's the best thing for all of you right now; you will see."

Joy looked at John intensely and said, "I just want to feel independent." Joy started feeling frustrated and needed to get away from John. She walked over to the couch and picked up Sophie to carry her into the room to put her to bed. She then came back for Sonya and placed her in the miniature crib John purchased for her.

John watched Joy as she walked away with Sonya and he smiled as he thought, *Ok, time for phase two of my plan because there is no way you are moving on without me. Everything is working out in my favor and this is the perfect time. After all these years, you will be mine before this is over.*

Joy glanced at John as she walked away. She thought about how he was such a good, dedicated friend. She wondered, like she had done so many times before, what his life was really like. He was always traveling somewhere for weeks at a time but always made time for her and Sophie if she needed him. He was quite handsome and a successful, prominent figure in the architecture industry, but that's all she really knew. Joy was never the type to pry into someone's personal life and knew this was a major flaw because that was why she couldn't find Sonya's father now.

John never spoke of his personal life. He just seemed to enjoy sitting around talking to her while spoiling the kids. Joy could tell he really loved children too, but he didn't have any of his own. He did so much for Sophie and Sonya that you would have thought he was their father. And although he wasn't their godfather either, he acted in a godfather's role. Joy thought once or twice that maybe, just maybe, he was a little interested in her. However, he never pushed forward with a relationship. Joy recalled when he made it clear the first day they met that he wasn't interested in a relationship. So Joy gave up on thinking he possibly wanted a relationship and accepted their closeness as just a close friendship. He became a regular figure in her life, to the point where they spoke almost daily. She even visited his small, one-bedroom apartment and wondered why such an established man would have such a humble place and didn't have a woman in his life. It was just all weird but Joy accepted it and as time passed, they just became closer. So Joy thought, *Why not stay at the hotel with him? Maybe we can connect like we never have before. Maybe, just maybe, I'll try to spark something myself. This may be my last chance before he returns to Juniper.* Joy walked back into the living room as John was taking some things out of his overnight bag. "I'm going back outside on the terrace for a while. I'm going to try to reach Charlene again to figure out these living arrangements ahead of time."

John looked up from his bag holding a pair of yellow silk boxers and an A-line tee shirt. "Ok babe, I'm just going to jump in the shower. It has been a long day."

Joy nodded her head as she thought, *Babe--he called me babe. Hmmmm...* She continued walking toward the patio door with her cell phone. Joy called and called but couldn't reach Charlene. She sat on the terrace for another fifteen minutes before she felt a little cold and decided to retrieve a sweater from her luggage.

As she entered the bedroom she could no longer hear the shower running, but she could smell John's body wash. The scent was alluring and she couldn't place the fragrance but it turned her on. She stopped in front of the bathroom door and continued to enjoy the scent of a real man after being alone for over a year now.

John opened the door abruptly and saw her standing there. "Oh I'm sorry, do you need to use the restroom, Joy? It's all yours. I'm done." John quickly walked past Joy into the living room to finish getting dressed. Joy didn't say a word as she watched him walk past her and down the hallway. His back and legs were sexy and strong. The dark hair on his legs was slicked down toward his ankles. He had a gold-colored jumbo Egyptian cotton towel wrapped around his waist and tucked tightly in the front. Joy could see through the slit of the towel wrap that he had already placed his boxers on in the bathroom. Joy watched him until he was completely out of sight and in the next room.

I guess I'll go shower now, she thought as she slowly entered the bathroom.

John could hear the shower start in the bedroom. He imagined the two of them taking a shower together and longed for that day. John pulled out the sleep sofa and prepared it for the night. He could have easily rented the top floor penthouse suite with plenty of room for all of them to sleep comfortably, but he knew money wasn't a driving factor for Joy. He didn't want to appear as though as he was trying to buy her affection, rather just help out here and there. They had never slept under the same roof overnight, although this was something John had secretly desired for the past few years. *It's just a matter of time,* he thought.

The room was quiet now and John figured Joy must have finished her shower. He called out to her but there was no answer. John needed linens for the sleep sofa so he walked into the bedroom to see if there were extra bed linens and a pillow in the closet. As he turned into the room, he caught a glimpse of Joy through the crack of the bathroom door. She was standing completely naked and her reflection in the mirror was heaven to his eyes. She still had a little of her baby fat from her last pregnancy but John thought she even more gorgeous with the extra weight. *I can't mess this up. I can't let her see me admiring her. I have to keep my cool until the time is right.* John quickly grabbed the full set of sheets and the pillow at the top of the closet and then left the room. He even closed the door to respect her privacy.

Joy stood in the mirror, looking at herself like she did often. *What is wrong me?* she thought. *Why can't I have a strong, responsible man like John as more than just a friend? Do I really want him to leave me here? He, my brother, and Susan are all I have had the past few years. If he's not spoken for, maybe I need to make the first move and step up from the friend zone instead of waiting on him to make a move. But what if that turns him off and he changes or leaves me like the rest have done?* Joy grabbed her head with both hands in frustration. *I need a drink to calm my nerves.*

Joy reached behind the bathroom door for a robe. She quickly slipped it over her naked body and exited the bathroom. She went straight into the kitchenette and poured herself a glass of vodka on the rocks. She drank the first glass straight down and then poured another. John was now lying down on the sofa bed. He appeared to be sleeping but Joy couldn't tell for sure from where she stood. Joy thought of going over to him then decided against it. *He doesn't want me. I'm just a charity case to him. If he wanted me he would have made it known by now. He's only doing this because of Sophie and Sonya.* Joy went back into the bedroom, checked on Sonya, and then lay down beside Sophie and fell asleep.

John could hear Joy in the kitchen pouring the alcohol that he did not want her to have. Drinking alcohol always reminded him of his wife, and he didn't want Joy to be anything like her. He knew Joy was stressed with this whole moving situation, but he was confident that he would be able to make all of them happy in the long run. He heard Joy exit the kitchen and head back into the bedroom. Everything was quiet for a while, so John headed into the bedroom to check on "his girls." Joy was lying beside Sophie. Joy still had her robe on and John could see that she wasn't wearing anything underneath. He was immediately turned on and could feel his erection taking control. He grabbed the covers and began to cover Joy and Sophie with the lightweight blanket. Joy shifted, causing her robe to fall fully open, exposing her supple breasts. John took one last look and thought, *One day, all of that will be mine to touch however and whenever I want.*

I've been waiting for years and I'll wait forever if I have to. John went back into the living room to the little sleep sofa and fell asleep.

Chapter 4 - Dawning of a New Day

JOY AWAKENED and realized it was now three in the morning. She could hear the television blaring from the living room where John was sleeping. She looked around the room in the darkness then jumped up and closed her robe that was revealing her nakedness. She walked to the miniature crib John had bought for Sonya and could see she was sleeping peacefully. So she went into the bathroom and brushed her teeth from the stale taste of the last glass of vodka she had drunk before she passed out on the bed. She checked her robe once again then walked into the living room where she admired John lying peacefully above the covers.

They had been friends for a little over two years and until now she never really looked at him like she did tonight. He had a strong bone structure and a muscular chest. His thighs were well formed and his manhood was quite present through his silk boxers. She moved closer and admired the fullness of his lips and began to feel her libido rising. She hadn't been with a man in over a year and had vowed to just stop dating until she got her life together. She walked back to the bedroom to check on Sophie and Sonya once more, then closed their door.

She returned to the sofa bed and gently slid in beside John. She had cuddled all the way into his armpit before he awakened to her presence. He looked in amazement at Joy, who was fully naked and lying under him. John thought he was dreaming and jerked away from her a little, then readjusted himself and asked Joy what she was doing. Joy put her finger over John's lips and crawled between his legs. John shifted as his manhood began to rise with the thought of Joy, of all people, placing her lips around the most private part of his anatomy. John quickly said, "You don't have to do this."

Joy didn't say a word. She knew what she wanted and right at that moment, she wanted to feel John inside her body in every way, starting with her mouth. She began to softly lick his engorged shaft and circled her tongue around the base as close to his body as possible. John looked down toward Joy and could see her beautiful naked frame and firm butt raised high in the air. John moaned in enjoyment as Joy sucked hungrily yet gently up and down his shaft while simultaneously rubbing his scrotum. She sucked and sucked while stroking him and could feel his veins thickening. Suddenly, she felt a vibrating sensation in her mouth and she knew that he wasn't far from exploding. Joy took him in as far as she could and then softly and slowly glided her mouth back up to the top.

John could feel himself at the peak of explosion and he gently lifted her head. John knew sex would be exciting with Joy but never imagined it would be like this from day one. John shifted positions and gently laid Joy down as she opened her legs, inviting him in. He couldn't wait to taste her sweet nectar. He had thought about this moment for years and couldn't believe she was the one to start it all. John lowered his head and took in her womanly scent, as he began massaging her with his tongue.

Joy shuddered at the feeling and enjoyed every moment of the pleasure John was giving her. John manipulated his tongue in ways that she would have never imagined. He knew just what to do to give her body the attention it had so desperately been missing. Suddenly he thrust his tongue deep inside her. Joy thought, *Is he tongue fucking me?* and gasped in satisfaction as she grabbed the back of his head. He held both of her legs high and grasped her thighs tightly, maintaining control of every movement. Everything felt so good and passionate, so wonderful and so right. Joy couldn't take it anymore as she experienced the orgasm of a lifetime. John watched her beautiful body tighten as he continued to slowly lick her until she no longer shivered. He wanted to ensure that she experienced pleasure like she had never known. Once Joy's breathing returned to normal, John climbed up to her as she grabbed his face and kissed him, while tasting her own sweetness on his tongue.

John's erection was rock hard and Joy was hot and ready for the finale. John positioned himself in a way that allowed easy access into Joy's center. He began to tease her with the tip of his erection and she began to throb in anticipation of what was coming next. She knew he delayed entering her on purpose to drive her crazy. Joy wanted him so badly right now and couldn't take it anymore, so she shifted her hips forward as he lowered his body more, and now she could feel his manhood, thick and warm, entering her. John was quite well endowed and he filled her completely. He could feel her center throbbing around him as he was deep inside of her. Their fingers intertwined as they entered into a faster rhythmic pace. When John felt he couldn't hold it any longer, he looked into Joy's eyes and said, "I love you, Joy Masterson.

I always have and I always will." Then he came intensely inside of her.

Joy shuddered in sheer satisfaction as she held him as tightly as she could. *Is this what I've been missing with John? Wow! He IS the whole package.* They both lay in complete silence. Joy thought of the amazing ecstasy that can only be achieved by two people making extreme passionate love like they just had as she fell asleep with even more positive dreams of a new beginning. In the meantime, John lay in sheer sexual satisfaction as he thought, *I can't believe this. How did this happen? She still doesn't know yet! I pray she forgives me.*

The week had passed quickly and Joy was ready to move on to her new life, and now she knew she wanted John to be a part of it. She had checked the college registration office to ensure her paperwork was all completed to start her classes. She was eager to finish her last year toward her Master's degree. She felt she was well on her way to becoming the Pharmacist she had always dreamed of being. Joy also found a job as a pharmaceutical sales representative and as a bonus, the job assigned her a personal vehicle. The job required experience but since she was in the pharmaceutical field, the hiring manager said he would give her a shot. Things were looking up in just one week, and she felt positive about her decision to make a change in venue.

John seemed different, though. Right after the night they made love, John left. He didn't speak much before he left; he just said he had to take care of some things and would return before it was time for them to check out of the hotel. She figured he must have been leaving to take care of some stuff at home but he never said exactly what he was doing. Sophie hated to see him leave and gave him a huge hug and kiss. She then made him promise to return soon. John promised her he would return and then he left.

In the meantime, Joy enrolled Sophie in school and found childcare for Sonya, who was going to stay with Charlene's mother Ruth for a while, until Joy got on her feet. She was happy that she no longer needed to find afterschool care for Sophie. Since her position was in outside sales, she was able to work around Sophie's school schedule. Joy hadn't been this happy in years. The only thing left to do was to contact the manager at the apartment complex where she had rented the apartment before this move to get a refund for her security deposit.

Charlene had suggested she and the children stay with her for the first year while Joy saved some money. Joy was considering the offer and was thinking of not contacting the manager at the apartment complex after all and just forfeiting the deposit. She could easily avoid the lease agreement she had signed because they failed to honor it anyway. John offered to help but she wanted to do as much as she could on her own. She really liked John and now saw him in a different light, but she still didn't want to owe anybody anything, including him. After being in an abusive marriage she knew living off of someone else could be difficult. She decided to take this new relationship with John slowly and still intended on paying him back every cent for the room he rented over the last week.

Joy finally met with Charlene and made a copy of the key to her apartment. Tomorrow was moving day and Joy was ready for it. The only thing missing was John, who promised to return before she checked out the hotel. If he wasn't back in time she would have to find someone to watch the children, drive the truck and move her things to Charlene's. John never failed her and she just knew he would be there in time to move her and the children's things. Unfortunately, this time she was wrong.

***

The morning after John and Joy made passionate love, John received a call from the hotel's office with a message to come to the front desk. He came to the front desk to find a uniformed officer and a plainclothes officer standing there. He rubbed his eyes as the uniformed officer stated, "Good morning, sir. Are you Mr. John Mack?"

"Yes, Officer. What is this about?"

"I'm Officer Freeman, and this is Detective Otis. Your wife filed a missing person report on you a few days ago in Juniper. Your credit card was traced here as the last transaction made."

"Oh, did she?" John began to chuckle then stated, "Well, you both can clearly see I'm not missing. She and I just had a disagreement, so I left."

"Ok sir. Well, can we see some identification so we can close this case? And please call her to let her know you are okay. She seemed very concerned."

"Yeah, I bet she is," John said as he looked in his wallet for his identification. He hesitated as he almost pulled out the wrong identification, then quickly recovered and handed the detective the correct one.

The detective glanced at the driver's license then handed it to the officer as he asked, "Are you here alone, Mr. Mack?"

John looked sternly at the detective and asked, "Why does that concern you, Detective? You have located me and that should be sufficient."

The detective started writing in his notebook as he stated, "So that means no."

Mr. Mack remained quiet as the uniformed officer handed him back his identification.

"Ok, sir. Have a nice day and I hope you two will be okay. Meaning you and your wife, that is," the detective stated as they headed out the hotel lobby.

"Yes, and you be safe out there as well," John said to the officer. John was pissed!

How dare that crazy bitch send the police after me? I need to send them after her! I told her to let this go but NOOO, she wants to play dirty, huh? John headed back to the room to shower and get dressed. He watched as Joy and the children slept peacefully and regretted that he had to leave them. He quietly retrieved a large white envelope from his overnight bag. On his way out he left the envelope at the hotel desk with special instructions to give it to Joy in two more days. He then headed back to Juniper to take care of Melinda once and for all.

Chapter 5 - Chance Encounters

TWO YEARS AGO...

JOY AND CHARLENE had always been close. They were second cousins who lived three hours away from one another. Charlene lived in Newcomb and Joy resided in Juniper. As they grew older Joy rarely had an opportunity to see Charlene, but after going through her divorce she decided to take a quick vacation to see her second cousin. Patrick and Susan volunteered to keep Sophie for the weekend so Joy packed her bags and took the three-hour drive. Charlene was at work when Joy arrived but insisted that they meet at Cantucci's, which was an upscale happy hour spot where many affluent people mingled. Joy would have never chosen to go there on her own. As Joy sat alone at the bar, she observed the crowd and noticed a rather handsome man who appeared to be popular with the waitresses and other patrons. He looked in her direction, obviously noticing she was a new face, then continued with his many conversations.

Joy glanced at her watch and contemplated leaving after not hearing from Charlene, until Carlos, the bartender, walked up and served her a glass of the finest wine Cantucci's offered. He told her the glass was bottomless for the night, compliments of Mr. Moss. Joy watched as Carlos nodded his head in the direction of a man standing a few feet away. The man nodded back to Carlos, held his glass up and nodded his head in the direction of Joy as if to say "cheers," then turned and continued to converse with a few of the other patrons.

"Mr. Moss, you say?"

Carlos nodded his head. "Yes, I thought everyone who came in here knew Mr. Moss."

"Well, I don't," said Joy. "Make sure you tell this Mr. Moss I said thank you." She grabbed her purse to tip Carlos, but he refused and stated, "Miss, that won't be necessary either."

About an hour had passed and Joy realized this Mr. Moss never formally introduced himself. Joy smiled and looked over to where she saw him standing last but he was no longer there. She tried to act like she wasn't looking for him as she excused herself to go to the ladies' room. She took an unnecessarily long trip around the lounge and she looked and looked but he was nowhere in sight. She returned to the bar, figuring he couldn't have left, then she indulged in a few more glasses of wine until she realized the generous gentleman still never approached her.

She finally asked Carlos if he knew where Mr. Moss could be and he answered, "Oh Miss, he has left for the night." Joy looked down at her glass and now realized she had drunk three full glasses of the sweet, delectable wine that she knew she couldn't afford. She glanced toward Carlos with a look of concern. He just smiled and said, "Don't worry; he left a special tab open just for you. So enjoy."

Joy felt thrilled that she didn't have to pay but a little embarrassed that she allowed Carlos to read her so well. She told Carlos thank you and left for the evening. She knew it was getting late and although Patrick and Susan didn't mind keeping Sophie, she didn't want to wear out her welcome.

Joy visited Cantucci's almost every evening looking for the mysterious Mr. Moss, with no luck. She'd only stay an hour or two then she would rush home to get Sophie or to work at the pharmacy. But after a few weeks she gave up and thought it was just a fluke. How could I get so interested in a man who dipped out on me after buying me a drink, and what kind of man never comes to introduce himself afterwards? she thought and laughed. Joy gave up on finding the mystery man until one evening as Joy was leaving the lounge, she felt a tap on her shoulder and a male voice asked, "Leaving so soon?" Joy turned around and saw it was the mysterious Mr. Moss.

"Hello, I'm Dwight, Dwight Moss, and your name is?"

"Hi Dwight, I am Joy. It is nice to finally meet you."

"Likewise!" he said.

She was ecstatic but tried her best not to show it. She finally got a good look at him, and he was very handsome. His head was full of thick, black hair that was perfectly cut short and tapered on the sides. His mustache was cut thin and it accentuated his full lips. His eyes were contoured and sexy, with long, dark lashes, and he had a strong, manly chin with light dimples when he smiled. He wore a finely pressed black suit jacket over an olive green shirt with no tie and a brown belt that matched his well shined, square-toed shoes that appeared to be about a size eleven.

Joy felt intimidated for a second until she gained her composure and retorted, "Well, maybe if a woman wasn't left in the dark after receiving such a fine glass of wine she would have a reason to stay."

Dwight loved the fire and confidence she so easily displayed. "Did you say, 'A glass of wine?' Because I was billed for much more than just 'a glass of wine.'" They laughed and talked all night long. That was the beginning of a beautiful relationship, or so she thought.

Joy and Dwight started dating on a regular basis whenever he came to town. Joy was happy that he didn't have a problem with her being a single parent, and he commended her for getting out of an abusive relationship. He was fun, spontaneous, ambitious and self-driven, always smiling and joking around, and Joy could see that people instantly loved to be around him. Dwight told Joy that his parents were real estate investors. He said he worked with them, along with his brother, right in Newcomb.

Joy told him that she lived three hours away in Juniper and to her surprise, Dwight said he also worked in Juniper from time to time. Joy wanted to introduce him to Sophie but wanted to wait until she thought they had a future together. However, one day they accidentally met when Susan brought Sophie back home after a quick afternoon at the mall. Sophie immediately bonded with Dwight and they all began to go out as a family whenever he came to town.

Over the next few months, the long distance relationship proved to be a challenge. Dwight rarely made it to Juniper due to his work schedule, but he always called her and visited her upon his return to town. Joy didn't know much about Dwight's personal life outside of their relationship. It made her feel uneasy, not knowing anything specific about his family or job. Joy often joked about not knowing any of his true friends and family members in hopes that he would open up and reveal a little bit more about his life to her, but that didn't work. She expressed to him one time that she thought he might be married with a family nicely stashed three hours away from her. Dwight would always laugh and say that one day he was going to take her to meet his entire family, and she would tell him, "Well, you better, because you know a girl that doesn't know her man's family and friends is nothing but his jump-off, right?"

Dwight would just laugh and say, "No baby. You're my future wife. I just have to make sure all the stars are pointing in the right direction when I reveal my queen to my world. Especially since I have your boy John sniffing around every corner now."

Joy found that Dwight always found a way to slide in a comment to express his distaste toward her and John's newly-formed friendship. Joy would normally just ignore his comments and carry on with their conversation. She knew Dwight wasn't going to say anything to John about their friendship. He would give Joy dirty looks whenever John contacted her, which was rare anyway. However, John's timing was awful. He always seemed to call when Dwight came to town and they were together. Joy never hid her friendship with John or her relationship with Dwight. She had no interest in John in a sexual manner at all at that time. He was more of a mentor and advisor to her life. Dwight wanted her to push John away; he suspected that John wanted a little more than just a friendship. However, Joy did not, but for some reason she just didn't want to shut John out of her life. He filled a void she had on an inner social level. His maturity, focus and attention to detail kept her captivated, so their relationship constantly grew

Joy remembered when she first met John. Joy was working the pharmacy counter when she received a call from Dwight.

"Hey, beautiful lady. What time do you plan on wrapping up tonight? Do you think your brother would mind watching Sophie all night? I have something really special planned for us."

"I'm sure Patrick and Susan wouldn't mind. They encourage me to get out of the house more. I'll call them, though, and let them know. Sophie should be already in bed anyway. I have to check inventory before I leave this evening, so it will be pretty late, maybe around 11pm."

"Okay. I'll be there by eleven to pick you up.

"I'll be right here as usual. Talk to you later."

Joy's back was turned from the pharmacy counter as she hung the phone on the receiver. She turned around and saw a tall, handsome man quietly standing at the counter waiting. If she hadn't known any better she would have thought Dwight was playing a trick on her because the man was almost the same height and build as Dwight.

"Well, hello. I'm sorry, sir, I didn't see you standing there. Can I help you?"

The man looked directly into Joy's eyes and appeared to just stare before he presented an all-too-friendly smile. Joy returned the smile but felt a weird uneasiness that she couldn't explain. The well-dressed man continued to flash his debonair smile.

"Can I help you, sir? Are you picking up or dropping off a prescription?" Joy asked more specifically, since the man didn't answer her the first time she asked him.

"Oh. Yes. Yes, I am," he said. The man continued to stare at Joy without giving additional information.

Joy looked perplexed and said, "Okay sir, uh, which one? Picking up or dropping off?"

The man began to chuckle a little and apologized. “I’m so sorry, your beauty is just breathtaking and I lost my train of thought.”

Joy smiled and blushed. “Well thank you, sir, now can I help you?

“Yes, of course. I’m dropping off this prescription for a sleep aid my doctor gave me. I haven’t been getting much rest these days on my own and you know what they say about getting enough rest.” He smiled at Joy once again as she took the prescription from him and asked for his identification to put him in the pharmacy's system. He pulled out his black soft leather Polo wallet and retrieved his driver’s license. As he handed her his identification he said, “Hello my name is John and I see by your name tag that your name is Joy. What a beautiful name for such a beautiful lady.”

Joy reached out and accepted the identification as she smiled and answered, “Well, thank you, John. Yes, I’m Joy,” she stated as she looked down and tapped her name tag. She then read his driver's license that identified him as Mr. John Mack of 222 Ellis Way Court. She looked up at Mr. Mack and thought he looked much younger than what his driver’s license showed. She actually thought he was about her age at first, but he was actually nine years older, making him forty-four.

“Ok, Mr. Mack, I'll take care of this for you. Would you like to wait for it or pick this up later?”

“Please. Call me John. How long will it be?”

“Let me check for you.” Joy said as she turned around and headed to the back of the counter to ask the Pharmacist. Joy returned to the counter and said, “It will be about an hour. Would you like to come back?”

“Okay, yes. I’ll do that. I have some other runs I need to make,” John stated as he thanked Joy and walked out of the pharmacy. About forty-five minutes later John walked back into the pharmacy. Joy was happy because it was the last prescription of the evening and she was ready to meet Dwight after they finished the inventory. Joy smiled at John as he approached and said, "Hello again."

"Perfect timing, John; your prescription is ready."

"Yes, perfect timing indeed," he stated as Joy handed him the prescription.

"And Ms. Joy, I didn't mean to be too forward, and I'm not looking for a relationship but I would love it if we could keep in touch some time." John simultaneously handed her his business card as he said the words "keep in touch."

Joy accepted the card that was practically thrust into her hand and stated, "Sure, I would love to."

John bowed his head a little at Joy and left the store. Joy looked at the business card she just accepted and couldn't for the life of her understand why she accepted it or even stated she would love to stay in contact with him. She smiled and shook her head as she placed the card in her work lab pocket.

Joy's co-worker Shay walked up to Joy at the counter and said, "I saw that!"

"You saw what?" asked Joy.

"I know him and I saw him trying to Mack on you! I should've known something was up because he's been in here three times this week and he doesn't normally come on this side of town."

"Girl, stop tripping. That man was getting a prescription filled and that was all," retorted Joy.

"Yeah, if you say so. But I know when a man is trying to Mack and Mr. Big-Time Architect Mack was trying to Mack on you," Shay said as she walked back to the rear of the counter to start filling prescriptions.

Joy discounted what Shay said and never thought twice about it. But she was curious about this John Mack and decided one day she might give him a call.

John's Version...

John sat in his car for almost an hour waiting to pick up his prescription. He had strategically parked his car all the way to the back of the parking lot but he faced the front door. From there he could see all the way to the pharmacy counter and had a full view of Joy as she worked. John thought about how sexy Joy looked as he watched her walk away, sashaying her perfectly curved hips and behind in her white pharmacy uniform jacket, to the back counter to ask the Pharmacist about the timeframe of his prescription being ready. He envisioned one day being able to place his hands around her slim waist and take her into his arms. It was 10:45pm now and the pharmacy was about to close. The whole time he sat in his car he tried to figure out a way to get Joy out of her everyday environment so he could get to know her better. He didn't want to seem like a pervert and didn't want his wife to find out either. But there was something about this woman he just had to know more about. He had to make her a part of his life, even if it were from afar.

As John was parked contemplating his next move on Joy he watched a black Mercedes Benz very similar to his pull into the pharmacy parking lot and park near the front door. The music from the car was blasting and he could vaguely see a man's head bobbing to the music through the tinted glass. The man just sat in the car and John began to focus his attention back on his true intentions with Joy. John decided to head back into the store. He knew he was about 15 minutes earlier than she advised him the prescription would be ready, but thought this would be a good opportunity to strike up a conversation. John walked up to the counter again. Joy saw him approaching and this time she smiled first. Yes! I'm in! he thought.

"Well hello again, beautiful," he said.

"Hiiiii John," Joy said.

John smiled and stated, "Look, I don't want to make you feel uncomfortable or anything. I'm not even trying to hit on you either, although you are quite beautiful. I actually work too much to sustain a real relationship, but honestly, I would like to get to know you better as a friend if that's okay with you." Joy looked bewildered as John thrust a business card toward her. Joy automatically accepted the card and said thank you as she read the front of the card, John Mack, CEO, Architect Dynamics Corp. "Is the prescription ready?" John asked, trying to act as casual as possible.

"Yes, it is. Let me get it," Joy answered as she walked to the back again to retrieve the prescription from the freshly filled ones on the Pharmacist's counter.

John knew what he was doing when he presented his card the way he did. He knew how to close a deal and normally the best way is to not ask; just tell the person and move forward. Only stop when and if they stop you, and she didn't stop him. She accepted the card and the offer and held on to it. Next, it would land in her pocket and she would call. Step one completed, John thought as a smirk spread across his face.

Joy came back to the counter with the prescription then she looked at the total. "Oh my, I'm so sorry, John, but I failed to enter your insurance information. Would you like me to take care of that for you now?" Joy asked.

"No thank you, dear, I'll put that on my card." John stated as he pulled out a black American Express Card.

"Okay, that's fine too," Joy said with a smile.

"Have a nice night, Ms. Joy. Hope to hear from you soon," John stated as he bowed his head and left the pharmacy once again. Joy smiled and said goodnight.

John walked back to his car and saw that the man in the other black Benz was still sitting in his car listening to his music. John got in his car and decided to wait around until Joy came out to find out what she drove. Another hour had passed and finally the pharmacy interior lights cut off. He could no longer see inside to the pharmacy counter and soon after the lights cut off, he could see several people leaving the store. John watched as everyone said their casual goodbyes and Joy walked toward a gold Honda Civic. She got in the car, moved it to another parking space and exited the car. She then walked toward the black Mercedes Benz and the driver jumped out and walked around to the passenger side and opened her door for her. John watched as Joy and the man shared a quick peck on the lips before she got in the car and they drove away. Competition, John thought as he followed the car until it was out of his sight. Hmmph! I expected that! Oh well, let the games begin.

Chapter 6 - Satisfying a Need

JOY STARTED to prepare the laundry when she found a business card in her lab jacket pocket. She read it and quickly remembered the handsome gentleman who insisted on her calling him John. *Wow, when was the last time I wore this jacket to work? I must not have worn this jacket in weeks,* she thought as she looked over the white uniform jacket. *Ohhhh, Dwight and I didn't come home that night and it was in that overnight bag I failed to unpack for over two weeks!*

She sat the business card on the dresser as she carried her laundry basket full of dirty clothes to the laundry room. She laughed at the thought of Shay telling her that the mysterious man was hitting on her. *Hmmm,* she thought. *He was a little interesting, though. Maybe I should give him a call. But how would Dwight feel about that? It's just a phone call, Joy,* she said to herself. *What harm could that cause?*

Joy looked at the time then walked to the dresser and retrieved the business card. She read the name aloud. "Mr. John Mack. It's not too early to call; it's after 12 noon," she muttered out loud trying to convince herself. Joy retrieved her cell phone and dialed the number on the business card.

"Hello. I'm trying to reach Mr. Mack."

"Yes. And may I ask who is calling please?" an older female voice asked.

"Ah, yes, it's the pharmacy. I would like to give Mr. Mack an update on his prescription," Joy lied.

"Please hold one moment. I'll see if he is available."

The lady put the call on hold for minute. Joy became nervous. *Why didn't he give me a direct number? I don't want to talk to his receptionist! I should hang up.* As Joy was about to hang up a male voice answered the phone. Joy could hear him thank the receptionist for transferring the call and then heard a click, confirming the transfer was complete.

"This is Mr. Mack. How can I help you?"

"Hello. This is Joy, from the pharmacy."

"Yes. I remember you, Joy. How are things going?"

All of a sudden Joy felt completely ridiculous for calling this Mr. Mack. She had absolutely no reason to call and he sounded like he was about all business.

"Ahhh, things are well," Joy answered. Then an awkward silence filled the phone for a few seconds.

John broke the silence. "Well Joy, I'm glad you called. Is there anything wrong with the prescription?"

"No, nothing is wrong with it. I just called on my own accord after finding your card in the laundry." Joy covered the phone and grimaced for telling him that his card was in the laundry.

"So you have hung me out to dry already and I haven't even gotten a chance to know you yet," John stated to relax the mood.

Joy laughed in relief at the comment. "No. I didn't hang you out to dry. I just forgot it was in my pocket. That's all."

"Well, how about you make it up to me and we have dinner this evening? That way you can tell me what's really wrong with my prescription. Considering that was the purpose of your call, right?"

Joy blushed at the request then laughed at the reasoning behind the dinner. "Sure, Mr. Mack, we can do that. I don't have classes this evening."

"I asked you to please call me John."

"Okay, Juh, Juh, Johnnnnn. Not a problem."

"Okay, that's better. I don't mean to sound like I'm rushing things but I have a few meetings to attend. It was a pleasure talking to you. And considering I do not have a way to reach you, I assume you will be contacting me again soon. Correct?

Joy hesitated then answered, "Well it would be easier if I had a direct number. I wasn't comfortable with the lady questioning the reason for my call."

"Sure, that's not a problem at all. I'll just give you my direct line. How does that sound?"

"That sounds better, John. I'll contact you later with a good time. I have to make sure I have someone to take care of my daughter.

"Oh, I didn't realize you had a daughter."

"Is that a problem?"

"No, no, not at all. Just surprised me a little, that's all.

"Well, yes, I come as a package deal!" Joy and John chuckled at her joke.

"Well I don't have any children, Joy, but I don't have a problem with them either."

"Ok, well that is wonderful," Joy said, feeling elated without knowing why.

"Enjoy your day, Joy."

John hung up the phone and Joy began to wonder even more about Mr. John Mack. Joy went to her closet and scrambled through her dresses in search of the perfect professional outfit for the evening. She settled on a simple black dress with low heels. Joy was excited about the evening but didn't consider it a date, really, or at least she was trying to convince herself it wasn't a date. It was more like a business meeting to her. Dwight was out of town on business with his family, as usual, and he wasn't scheduled to return to town for another week. Joy thought it wouldn't be a good idea to hide the fact that she was going out with John. So she decided to make a call to Dwight.

"Hey Dwight, how is business?" Joy asked as she folded some tee-shirts from the first load.

"Busy," Dwight answered flatly.

"Okayyy. Am I bothering you? Or did I call you at a bad time?"

"No. I'm just trying to take care of some stuff and I need to make a few runs, that's all."

"A few runs? Meaning?" Joy asked.

"Look, not right now, Joy. I'm not dealing with this right now."

"Dealing with what?" Joy asked calmly. "All I asked you was how is business going? Then you tell me you need to make a few runs. So I ask what the heck does making a few runs mean and you go ballistic on me."

"Joy, you take everything to heart. Stop being so sensitive."

"I'm not taking anything to heart and I'm not being sensitive. You are being elusive and that makes me feel like you have something to hide."

"I don't have anything to hide from anybody. I don't have to explain myself to anyone."

"I got to go, Dwight. I just called to tell you I was going out with a friend later on tonight but go ahead and handle your 'few runs.'" Joy hung up the phone, frustrated with how

Dwight easily flipped to this mean, arrogant, selfish, uncaring person when she least expected it.

Joy thought, *Here I am calling him to tell him what's up with me and he's acting like a complete ass. But he's right; he doesn't have to tell me anything, so why am I telling him everything?* Joy began to cry at the harshness in his voice as she prepared the next load of clothes for the washer. *He doesn't understand how much I truly love him and just want him to see things my way sometimes. He is simply pushing me to someone else.* Joy finished her and Sophie's laundry and eagerly got ready for her evening with Mr. John Mack.

Joy drove up the mountainside to meet John at an elegant restaurant named La'Cliffe. "There she is," John stated to the hostess as he pointed in Joy's direction then headed to greet her at the door. She watched as John signed a paper at the door prior to entering the restaurant, then asked her to sign as well.

"Uh, what is this before I sign it?" Joy asked.

John smiled and said softly, "This is a very exclusive restaurant. This form is a confidentiality agreement that we do not speak of anything or anyone we see in this establishment or we could be sued."

"Okayyyyyyy," said Joy. "They wouldn't get much out of me anyway so sure; I'll sign."

John looked at Joy as she signed the confidentiality agreement and wished his wife had the same fun, free spirit she possessed.

They entered the foyer, and Joy was in absolute awe of the beautiful setting. She had been to several nice restaurants in town with Dwight but had never even heard of this place. The entire restaurant literally sat on the edge of the mountain's cliff. She guessed that explained its name.

Everything was black and white marble. The flooring was made with large, three by six foot slates of transparent glass between solid marbled black flooring. It almost made you want to jump from slate to slate to avoid walking on the transparent sections. You could see clear to the bottom of the mountain, making you wonder how it was constructed. There was a huge black piano in the center of the room with a pianist taking requests. The individual table settings were all alongside the window and placed on the transparent section of glass. There was a curtain available to make your setting even more private. A few of them were already closed and Joy wondered what was going on behind those curtains. The ambient lighting from the candle set the scene as you looked upon the distant body of water beyond the adjacent mountain's view. John smiled casually at Joy and asked, "Is this okay?"

"Yes. But it's a little much. You think?" Joy asked.

"Only if you value yourself and your time as less." John looked at Joy and waited for a response, but she didn't respond. The hostess escorted them to their private seating.

Two hours had passed, and Joy found that John brought a distinctive edge to her life. John never truly flirted with her. Joy couldn't understand why he never flirted, considering when they first met he spoke of how beautiful he thought she was. Instead, they just talked while enjoying their meals and instantly the platonic nature of their new friendship strengthened their bond. Joy welcomed the inspirational conversation. His thought processes were so motivationally driven that it inspired her to rethink her passion for opening her own pharmacy one day. John appealed to her mentally like no other man had. They talked about mind tantalizing topics, not just everyday mojo, and she knew she wanted more. They talked just a little about his business and a lot about her college studies and future goals. She spoke of how hard her classes were and what it actually took to become a

Pharmacist. John didn't realize that a Pharmacist was actually a doctor or that it required so much schooling. He admired her tenacity, given that she was a divorced, single parent and didn't have the support and financial backing that most people have. Joy remembered being nervous to call John but was now glad that she had.

"You know, I was scared to call you at first," Joy said.

"Why?"

"Well, I'm in a relationship and I thought you were hitting on me." Joy laughed. "But a woman could get used to this treatment."

"I'm glad you called, Joy. Like I said, I work a lot and don't have a lot of time to settle down with a relationship. But I did want to get to know you better. Becoming friends first is better anyway. Don't you agree?"

"Yes. I agree," Joy said. "I just can't believe someone hasn't snatched you off the market yet," she laughed.

"Well, you can't be snatched if you don't want to be snatched," John said as he looked away from Joy and onto the mountainside. *I wish I had never been snatched,* he thought. "Would you like anything else?"

"No. Everything has been great. Especially the conversation."

"Well, let's get down this mountainside. I feel bad that you drove all the way here by yourself. But I will follow you to make sure you make it home safely."

"That won't be necessary, John. I'll be just fine. And I'll call you in the morning," Joy stated confidently.

John said, "Ok Madame, as you wish." John told the waiter to put the bill on his account and they left for the evening.

The entire drive home, Joy thought of her evening with John: the wonderful restaurant he was willing to take her to with no strings attached, the no-pressure atmosphere and, of course, the unselfish topics and conversation. She thought about how although she enjoyed Dwight, he didn't seem interested in what she wanted out of life. She found Dwight constantly talking about himself and the growth of the company he was starting with his brother. But she noticed that his future never seemed to include her in it. He would go on and on about how he wanted to come out completely from under his family's real estate investing company and use all of his proceeds to start his own company. He talked about how successful he planned to be. He spoke of building a huge company and traveling the world. He talked of how he would like to donate to charities and churches by building homeless shelters and group home facilities.

And Joy had always supported his ventures. She had even researched a few things for him during her limited free time. But instead of discussing the information she located to help him get the ball rolling with her, he would confer with someone else and then execute a plan without her. At times she felt slighted when it came to his interests, especially when she discovered he found solace in someone else's opinion over hers. Joy tried to ignore her feelings in this area by trying to express her dreams and desires to run her own pharmacy department or even open her own pharmacy. She wanted him to support her like she supported him. But instead he didn't seem interested in her dreams at all. It would be a dead-end conversation, with no input at all from Dwight's perspective. Joy thought she loved Dwight but also thought this was a very selfish part of him. Instead of expressing her feelings about it, she just dismissed her negative thoughts and continued to listen and support him with whatever he needed whenever he needed it. But this alone was a driving force to continue to communicate with John. He seemed to be genuinely interested in what she wanted as well, and she needed that support in her life. He was definitely satisfying a need within her and she decided no matter how Dwight felt about their friendship, she was not going to let John go.

Chapter 7 - Who is John Mack

THE INFAMOUS man known to everyone as Mr. John Mack sat in the little living room of the hotel suite and thought about the past few years of his life. He was where he wanted to be right now with Joy and Sophie but didn't really know how to get out of his current situation with his wife and her family.

John had a troubled and violent childhood. He was adopted at fifteen and grew up with a middle class family as their only child. He watched his adoptive parents work hard at odd jobs for everything they earned. He learned a lot from them about the value of money and hard work. He was a gifted child and was placed in advanced placement classes throughout high school and college. By thirty he had permanently moved to Juniper and was the best young architect in the region. He was single, young, smart, ambitious and handsome--just what any company needed to land major deals and keep them on top of the industry. Soon he was head-hunted by the best architecture companies across the region and ended up employed at The Architect Dynamics Corporation (ADC).

The Conglin family owned ADC and they had connections from the east to the west coast and even abroad. John was now making well over six figures as a lead designer for local projects but the owner and founder of ADC, Mr. Matthew Conglin, saw more potential in John than the rest of his colleagues that had been recently recruited. So Matthew invited John to his private estate for an informal meeting and that's where John met Matthew's daughter and his future wife, Melinda. Melinda was strikingly beautiful, amazingly glamorous and just outright stunning. John had a weakness for physically attractive women and when she walked into the Matthew's home office, John's eyes lit up.

John could not help but stare at the beautiful woman as she continued to walk across the room with her fair-colored skin and full, soft-looking head of curls that flowed down her back, framing her slender face. She wore too much makeup for John's liking, but was still gorgeous with full, pouty lips. She had on a tailor-made skirt suit that hugged her curves perfectly and showed off her long, shapely legs as she strode across the room with poise and confidence.

He immediately wondered who she was. Matthew noticed John's attraction to his daughter and immediately introduced the two. Melinda said hello, spoke with her father briefly then sashayed out of the office as John and Matthew turned back toward each other to continue their meeting. John wanted to visually follow her so that he could continue to indulge in her beauty but out of respect for her father thought that wouldn't be wise.

Matthew talked about his vision for the future of ADC and wanted John to be a huge part of it. John was highly interested but had been distracted since laying eyes on Melinda. He didn't want his interest in her to seem obvious, so he found another way to approach the subject and asked

Matthew if he had any sons who could help him run the business. Matthew explained that Melinda was his only child and she lacked the experience needed to run the business, to his dismay.

John was astonished that Melinda was the only heir to Matthew Conglin's sixty million dollar fortune. Suddenly, she became even more interesting to John and he hoped she would return again. However, he and Matthew talked for hours and Melinda did not resurface.

At the end of the meeting, John said his goodbyes to Matthew and the estate staff as he exited the grand foyer. As he got into his car, his cell phone rang and he recognized the number as that of the Conglin estate. John immediately answered, thinking he might have left something inside, only to discover it was Melinda.

"Hello. Mr. Conglin?" John stated as he answered his phone.

"No. But you could say Ms. Conglin if you like," answered Melinda.

"Well, hello, Ms. Conglin. To what do I owe the pleasure of this call?"

"I found you quite interesting, John. My father has had many new architects before but never brought them home like a pet. He must really like you or you have something great to offer, or is it both?"

John hesitated and thought, *Did she just refer to me as her father's pet?*

"Well, Melinda... Oh, excuse me. Is it ok for me to call you Melinda?"

"As long as you're not the staff and for now, sure."

John hesitated again and thought, *This chick is really feeling herself. What a turn-off.*

"Well, ok, ME-LIN-DA... for now," he repeated sarcastically. "What's going on with you? Did I leave something at the estate?"

"No. But I figured you may want to take me out to dinner one day soon. I'll be available tomorrow and you can see me at 8pm. I love a really well-prepared filet mignon, so I also have a place in mind."

John remained quiet.

"Hello?" Melinda spoke into the phone then looked at it to see if her call had disconnected and saw it hadn't.

John sat silently holding the phone in his car with a smirk on his face. He was initially physically attracted to Melinda but after their brief conversation, he instantly lost his attraction to her. "I'm here," John said. "Look, I don't think dating the boss' daughter is exactly a good idea. So how about we keep this relationship strictly professional?"

If he could've seen her face, he would have known how distraught she was that he wanted to remain professional. Melinda started fuming at the disrespect she felt behind him turning down her proposal. She thought, *No one turns me down! Who the hell does he think he is? I am Melinda Conglin!*

Melinda gained her composure and calmly responded, "I understand completely, John. I'm sure you're quite intimidated by my father, like many have been in the past. However, I assure you an amicable relationship between you and me could prove to be rewarding in a number of ways. I'll see you tomorrow at my estate at 8pm. Goodnight, Mr. Mack."

John heard the phone disconnect and knew Melinda had given him an ultimatum. He knew this could affect his relationship with Matthew and his position at the company. *How do I play my cards on this?* He shook his head and thought of how much trouble getting involved with her could be or what would happen if he didn't agree to her request. *How much power can she really have? She's not even in the business!* John stressed all night over what to do. *I'll decide in the morning!*

After a short and restless night, John dressed for work and went to his office. He walked past the line of cubicles and remembered when he once sat in one of those seats striving to get where he was now. Once in his office, he saw a large black envelope labeled with his name. He wasn't expecting any information from clients and couldn't find a return label to identify the sender. Instead of just opening the envelope, he walked out of the office to the front desk and asked the young receptionist, who received all the incoming mail, if she knew who had left the unidentified black envelope. She stated she had no idea.

John thanked her then walked back to his office. He stared at the envelope again. It was made from high quality paper and smelled of soft rose petals. John thought, *I know she didn't,* as he used a stainless steel envelope opener to see what was inside. He pulled out a full itinerary Melinda had prepared for their date that evening. John sat down at his desk as he looked over the plans she made, including limousine service to and from the restaurant she chose. She included black tie services and had his tuxedo scheduled to be delivered so he would be properly dressed for their evening. *What makes her think I'm wearing a tux tonight? She is about to be terribly disappointed!* She ended the itinerary with a note for him to call her upon receipt of this envelope. John chuckled at the forwardness of it all and couldn't believe Ms. Melinda Conglin was soooo interested in Mr. Rags to Riches himself. *If only she knew who I really am.* He had no intention of calling her as she wished but thought, *Ok, I'll play along with your bossy demands, Melinda. I'll make this worth my time and your dime in the end,* as he balled up the linen paper and tossed it into the wastebasket.

A year later, John and Melinda were the talk of the company. He had landed the boss' daughter and she was head over heels for him. John learned that Melinda was correct when she told him that dating her had its perks and yes, it did. His career catapulted within the company. He became Matthew's right-hand man and the more established he became in the company, the more he secretly hoped Matthew would never learn of his past. John dated Melinda for over a year but they had never had sex because she wanted to wait until they got married. Melinda stated that mantra over and over like it meant something to John, when he didn't desire to have sex with her at all anyway.

Matthew often spoke of all the things from which John could benefit by marrying his daughter. He offered him the position of Deputy CEO and his salary of $150,000 a year would increase exponentially, making John an automatic millionaire with access to all funds and personal expense accounts. John couldn't believe the offer and was ready to jump on it while it was hot on the table.

There was one major problem; he didn't love Melinda. He didn't even like her as a person. He continued to date her but John never loved her the way a man should love a woman he planned to marry. He found her to be selfish, vain, and rotten to the core. He hated the way she treated the staff at the estate and when they went out to restaurants, she always complained rudely to the waiters or waitresses about her food. John started to purposely take her to places to ensure they had waiters to serve them because she was extra rude to the waitresses. One evening she literally tossed her bowl of soup at a pretty young waitress and complained that it was cold. Then she had the nerve to turn around and smile at John like it was okay. John grimaced at her because he knew she only did that because she was jealous of the waitress' beauty, so she attempted to disgrace the young beautiful waitress in front of everyone. Her actions were totally unnecessary because she was also quite beautiful. John knew there was nothing wrong with her soup at all. Melinda just wanted to be superior to every other being that she assumed wasn't in her tax bracket and it annoyed John to the utmost, especially since his adoptive mother used to serve tables just to send him to a decent school. He wondered how Melinda would act if she was aware of this.

John also despised how she constantly slung her family's name around, attempting to justify her self-entitlement and rudeness just because her family's name represented power around town. The Conglin name made things happen that should never occur and people's careers disappear like they never existed. John thought about his upbringing and never wanted to return to that life, and after learning of the benefits of becoming Melinda's husband, he decided to marry her.

It was a huge, elaborate wedding with trimmings and guests from all over the world. John was dressed and ready to stand before the pastor when Matthew walked into the dressing area with a man he introduced as his attorney, but to John he looked more like an enforcer. Matthew excused the groomsmen then asked John to have a seat. John was familiar with most of Mr. Conglin's staff but had never met this particular attorney before. The attorney opened his briefcase and presented John with some pre-filled documents. John looked confused as the attorney handed him a pen and asked him to sign beside the X. John was surprised and insulted at the same time when he saw in bolded letters at the top of the document, "Prenuptial Agreement." Mr. Conglin looked directly at John and stated,

"I know all about you." John began to sweat in fear of the worst. "You came from nothing and my only daughter loves you. So if you decide to leave her or hurt her in any way you will leave the same way you came. Understand?" The attorney forcefully slid the paperwork closer to John.

John thought of the over 5,000 guests of the Conglins who were patiently seated right down the hall from his dressing area and the $300,000-plus bill to make this wedding magical. John thought of how Mr. Conglin must have strategically planned to serve this prenuptial agreement just minutes before the wedding to eliminate the possibility of him walking away and not going through with the wedding. He also wondered if she was aware of this deal. As John looked into Mr. Conglin's eyes, he knew that this was a blood deal and he was selling his soul. John didn't even read the papers any further. He just signed the document in the indicated spot and walked out the door as he thought, *No Matthew, you don't know everything about me. You don't have a clue! Yeah, I'll marry your prissy-ass daughter and take your money in the process. I'll find a way to end up with everything I want.*

Minutes later Melinda was walking down the aisle. John stood before the pastor, knowing he was telling lies of loving and cherishing this woman until death do them part. John looked at her. She was physically flawless. She wore a beaded pure white dress that perfectly contoured her breasts in a V-neck pattern. The fabric fit snugly around her slim waist and contoured around her hips and buttocks. The actual dress ended mid-thigh over her shapely legs but had a silken ultra-sheer material that extended to her ankles. The back was embellished with a huge bow that outlined the crease of her back. The tails of the bow formed into a lightweight train that flowed beyond her ankles. Her veil was also pure white, with pearl and rhinestone trimmings that anyone would have sworn were diamonds. Again, she was completely flawless and any man would salivate over her physical beauty.

John was a victim to her physical beauty until he learned she had nothing else to offer him besides money and power. John was used to a woman who at least tried to cook and clean. She had done none of the above at all in their year long relationship. She thought that was beneath her. He tried to have intelligent conversations with her but although her father sent her to the finest schools her interests were lacking anything meaningful. If she wasn't discussing the gym, hair, nails or shopping, the conversation was fruitless.

The reception immediately followed the wedding and John felt like he was in a trance. He watched all the smiling faces, hugs and handshakes given to her father. John felt a new strong resentment for a man he thought he had become close to over the past year. He felt he had been completely ambushed with the prenuptial agreement. All the respect he had for her father died that day. Although he was marrying her for all the wrong reasons, he felt his work and merit should count for itself and not be subject to threats with a failed marriage.

As the reception came to an end John and Melinda were chauffeured to her father's private jet. They flew to Bora Bora for their honeymoon.

Chapter 8 – The Dark Side

JOHN FELT LIKE he was in a trance as Melinda snuggled under him, interlocking her arms with his like he was her prized possession. John thought of how sex would be with Melinda, knowing how controlling and uptight she was. He still hadn't sampled her merchandise yet and she was always proud to tell people that she was making him wait. John wanted so much to tell everyone that he didn't want her or it anyway, but thought of how revealing his true feeling about Melinda could ruin this glamorous lifestyle he had practically stumbled into.

When they arrived in Bora Bora they were pampered with dual massages and served fresh fruit and expensive wine. During the massage, John glared at the new Mrs. Conglin-Mack. Melinda refused to drop her maiden name and chose to hyphenate it instead. She seemed so happy and was quite talkative even though John wasn't responding to anything she said. Her conversation was like it always was, closed-ended, meaningless and uninformative.

Melinda felt John staring at her and smiled as if she were flattered. John didn't blink. Melinda finally asked, "Is everything okay, dear?"

John continued to glare at Melinda and then asked, "Did you know about the prenuptial agreement your father had me sign just minutes before we were to be married?" He hoped she didn't know. He prayed she would say no. He wanted to make something out of this terrible relationship and figured time would help him to love this woman in whom he had no interest whatsoever but to his surprise, she didn't even hesitate to answer as she smiled and responded, "Of course."

She raised her wine glass and then stated, "But that doesn't matter anyway, right?" John looked away from her. He was fuming and didn't respond at all.

They both lay quietly while completing their massages and headed back to their villa. Melinda changed into a sexy red lingerie ensemble. He had never seen anything besides her cleavage and legs up to now. Her body was beautiful and she was sexy but his mind could not get over her manipulative ways. John knew it was time to consummate their marriage and felt he needed to loosen up with a stiff drink. She sashayed around the room to the large mirror, where she brushed her hair and checked her makeup. She handed John a bottle of champagne to open and poured herself a huge glass. John was completely sober and headed to the bathroom while Melinda drank glass after glass of the champagne. John stood in the bathroom and could hear her as she beckoned for him to return and taste what he had been waiting for all year. John enjoyed oral sex but the notion of pleasing her in that way made him feel like her two-bit sex slave just because NOW she was ready. John looked toward the bathroom door and thought, *If anything,*

I'll stick my dick in her mouth first. John figured there was no more running from this and exited the bathroom. Melinda was stretched across the bed and had fallen asleep. He looked at her beautiful body but wasn't aroused because he was so angry at the deception he felt he endured. Instead of waking her, he stood over her and drank the entire second bottle of champagne straight from the bottle. Then he got dressed and walked out of their private villa to the resort's beach party.

John physically shuddered at the thought of what happened next. He always shuddered when he thought of what occurred the night of his wedding. He tried many times to erase it from his memory but knew that wasn't possible. The memory always crept back into his mind and there it was again, haunting him, replaying in his head. The beach party, the hotel room, even the smell of the woman's cigarettes on her body were all fully recollected in John's mind.

The darkness of that day began again as John remembered the beach party he attended that night. It was full of lively people he knew his wife would feel were beneath her. There were half-clad beautiful women of all ages scattered everywhere. John leaned on a wooden carving dressed in white linen shorts and a button-down linen shirt. He drank several rum punch concoctions. The more he drank the angrier he became as he thought about his situation with his new wife. He thought of her lying there waiting for him to have sex with her for the very first time. But he had no desire to touch her at all.

Instead he eyed a pretty young woman who had been watching him since he arrived at the beach party. Before he could wink an eye, they were in her room and he was deep inside of her. With every angry stroke he thought of his new wife and how he could disgrace her like she had done so many people in his presence. He thought of her father and the degrading pre-nuptial agreement he was practically forced to sign. He thought of his life and everything else except the fact that he was having sex with some stranger he just met on the beach on his honeymoon. *I'm just another piece of her property,* John thought.

The woman moaned in pain and pleasure as John penetrated her deeper and deeper and he became rougher and rougher with each stroke. The woman looked at John as his expression completely changed from a nice professional guy to a deranged lunatic. His eyes were red and bulging and his teeth were clenched as he angrily entered her over and over again. When he started to pound her violently she tried to grip the sides of his hips to make him stop or at least slow down, but he would not stop. To John everything was black. He no longer saw anything or felt anything. John's secret violent past slowly crept into his new life with every violent stroke she took. It didn't matter how she felt or how she looked up at him.

Suddenly, John grabbed the woman by her throat as she tried to scream for him to stop. Her face turned red in fear as he continued to pound and pound between her legs until he pulled out and ejaculated all over her chest and face. The woman tried to move but John had her pinned to the bed. He watched her strangely as she lay quietly, waiting for his next move. The woman watched as John's expression changed back to the normal nice professional guy. He now realized he wasn't pounding the cold bitch he married and that he must have blacked out. The woman looked terrified beneath him. John wiped away his sperm from her face and body with the bed sheet. He leaned over and kissed her gently on the forehead and said, "I'm sorry I was so rough, but thank you. I needed that."

The woman's face softened and she looked confused as John got up and grabbed his wallet. She slowly got up as well and staggered to the bathroom in obvious pain. When she returned

John was gone and all she saw was a wad of money on the dresser. She walked over to the dresser to count the money and saw ten one hundred dollar bills. She smiled and said, "Well damn, I'm not even a prostitute. I guess that was worth that painful fuck. I'll catch up with him later, I'm sure." Then she headed back in the bathroom to shower.

John arrived back to his private villa where he found his wife was still sleeping. She was now lying on her stomach with one leg up and John could see her black and red thongs between her legs. He dropped his pants and stood over her as he stroked his penis until it was extra hard. He spat on his hand to lubricate his penis then climbed on top of her back, yanked her thong to the side and thrust his penis into her vagina. He dropped all his weight on her as she tried to wiggle away from the uninvited attack. John leaned in close to her ear and said, "Is this what you been waiting for you cold hearted bitch? You thought you were going to dictate my dick too, didn't you?"

She didn't respond and stopped trying to fight as John continued his assault. "You're nothing but a spoiled little prissy bitch! How dare you make ME sign a pre-nup! I should get paid for marrying your good for nothing ass. Oh, my fault--your family is rich so you are good for one thing, huh!" She could smell the stale, strong stench of sex and alcohol on his breath. She also caught a whiff of an unknown, cheap female fragrance. She could feel the intensity of his anger and knew she had pushed him too far with the pre-nuptial agreement. She remained quiet as John continued his verbal and physical tyrant. With every stroke he seemed angrier and angrier.

"You have been dictating this relationship and my business dealings with your father from day one and you knew I didn't want your ass in the first place! I have been your little bitch this whole year, from what I ate to what I drank to what I wore when I was with you! Well, you couldn't control this could you, Melinda? You wanted me to eat you out, didn't you! Well, how about I make YOU suck my dick! I can't stand you prissy ass, but I think I finally found one thing I like about you and that's your mouth shut and your ass up just like this, answering to ME!" He stopped for a second and grabbed both her wrists then snatched both her arms back, giving him full control of every movement and every inch of his huge penis entering her as he continued to stroke her from the back. Melinda tried to break free as she squealed and winced in pain until John finally came inside her. He released her wrists and her chest collapsed to the bed. John got up as Melinda slowly rolled over and looked directly in his eyes.

She could see the hatred he had for her in his eyes. They were as red as fire and hard to the core. They both sat in silence as both digested what had just happened. Melinda broke the silence as John got up and headed to the bathroom. "Did you just rape me?" John remained quiet and kept walking away from her. "Really, John. What the hell was that? Why do you smell like stale liquor, cigarettes and pussy?" John turned around and blankly stared at her as she spoke.

"Did you leave our villa? Did you sleep with another woman on our honeymoon then rape me? Do you hate me that much?" John never answered. He shook his head and slowly started walking again. As he walked away she stated, "I know what's wrong with you. You don't love me. You're in love with my family's money." John stopped in his tracks but didn't look toward her. Her voice changed to a deeper, more sinister tone as she stated, "You will learn to love me just like you love my money. Just wait and see."

John looked back at her this time. She was lying on the bed exhibiting a diabolical expression. She gazed at him as he turned around and proceeded into the bathroom and slammed the door. John was eager to get in the shower to wash off both of the women he had just had sex with. The hot water trickled down the glass door and the bathroom was full of steam. John's anger turned to despair as he began to cry. He asked himself, "Why did I agree to this marriage. I should have walked away. Why was I so greedy?" The water began to run cold after John stood in the same spot for close to an hour. "I have to make this right or give this marriage a try. That's what I'll do, I'll try." John stepped out of the shower and dried his face and body as he mentally prepared to start his new life with his new wife.

Chapter 9 – Let's Make This Work

THE MORNING AIR was refreshing and a crisp, light breeze came through the villa's windows. John rubbed his eyes as he rolled over in search of Melinda, who was nowhere to be found. He frowned and smacked his lips from the stale, leftover alcohol taste that lingered there from the night before. "Linda," he called out into the empty room. There was no answer. "Linda," John called a little louder this time, but again there was no response.

John jumped up and glanced out the window. The view of the water was gorgeous. He checked his watch on the dresser; it was 7:30am. John thought of where Melinda could be and then recalled her mentioning she couldn't wait to take a run on the beach. John showered and dressed but Melinda still had not returned so John left the villa and headed to the little restaurant for breakfast and some coffee.

As he walked into the tropically designed café he spotted his wife already seated, having breakfast with someone. The stranger's back was facing John as he approached the table.

Melinda looked up from her guest and stated, "Good morning, honey. The coffee is awesome. Would you like to join us for a cup and something to eat?"

The stranger turned around to say hello to John and to his surprise, it was the woman he had sexual relations with the night before. The woman spoke to John like she had no idea who he was. John didn't know what was going on and remained silent.

"John, is something wrong? Melinda asked.

"Uh, no but I'm not really hungry. I was just checking on you."

Melinda cut her eyes at John and said, "Come on now, I'm sure you could use something to eat after the night you had. Why don't you join me and ummmm... what's your name again, dear?" she asked the woman sitting with her.

"OH, yes, I'm Madeline," the lady quickly replied.

"Yes, that's right Ma-DE-Line." Melinda pronounced every syllable of Madeline's name as she slowly turned her head back toward John.

John instantly knew she knew something. John just wasn't sure what she knew but either way, he wasn't going to entertain the notion. "No, thank you, dear. I'm going back to the villa for room service. I think I will stay in all day and tonight."

Melinda looked at John as she squinted her eyes at him and said, "Yeah, you do that. I'll meet you there a little later." John didn't say a word as he walked the long way back to their villa.

Melinda didn't come back to the villa for several hours. John was sleeping peacefully when she returned. She began to pack all of their things as she glared at him about what she had learned of his last night's encounter with Madeline. After learning of his late-night escapade she didn't know what she wanted to do. She was so embarrassed when Madeline calmly told her that that was the man she told her about earlier in their breakfast. She and Madeline had met in the gym that morning and decided to have coffee. Madeline asked Melinda if she enjoyed the beach party the night before. Melinda said she didn't attend but asked how the party was. Madeline wasn't ashamed to tell Melinda in full detail about her romp in the hay with a stranger and when Melinda put two and two together, she realized it was Madeline that John had slept with right before he slept with her last night. Melinda was disgusted but kept her composure so she could gain as much information as she could. She even gave Madeline a business contact card to gloat about her family's business. However, she later regretted going that far and prayed Madeline would never contact them in the future.

Melinda thought of leaving the resort then changed her mind over another bottle of champagne. Instead, she plopped herself down in a chair across from John and watched him sleep. John awakened to Melinda just staring blankly at him. She was looking beautiful wearing nothing but a small, simple tee shirt and some thongs while seated in a small grey plush chair adjacent to the bed. John looked up at Melinda, who continued to stare directly at him. Instead of the stuck-up, privileged, spoiled brat he had known the past year, he saw a plain, simple, hurt woman. Her usually make-up matted face was fresh and clear. Her eyes were not completely consumed with mascara and eye shadow, her hair was neatly and naturally flowing down her back. She wasn't sitting perfectly and poised in the chair as she had always done. She was as plain as ever and John had never appreciated her beauty more than that moment. The room remained quiet as John slowly raised himself off the bed and went to the bathroom to brush his teeth. He came back into the room and stood behind her in the chair. She could feel his presence, but she didn't move. John slowly walked around to face her then lifted her from the chair. Melinda didn't resist. He gently laid her on the bed as he admired her beauty from head to toe. For the first time he leaned toward her and began to kiss her because he actually wanted to. Melinda still didn't resist. John slowly rubbed her thigh, then removed her thongs. He slowly lowered his lips between her legs to her lips and gave her what she so desired until she burst into satisfaction. Then they made love for the first time. Afterwards, no sounds were made and no words were said as they silently drifted to sleep in each other's arms.

Chapter 10 - Mrs. Melinda Conglin-Mack

MELINDA MET JOHN when she was 33 years old and now she and John had been married for three years. When they married she knew he didn't love her and didn't want to be with her. She knew from day one that her affluent status and the way she acted toward the staff bothered him. She also knew he never wanted to date her in the first place, but her father Matthew was terminally ill and Melinda had to find a suitable mate to take care of her and run the business.

John was the talk of the company amongst the women. Melinda was used to having the best, so if he was the best in the litter of her father's architects she was determined to make him hers. She attempted to tempt him with the luxuries and the status of being a part of the Conglin family, but that didn't seem to impress him. She exposed him to elegant gatherings and conventions that only the top executives of Fortune 500 companies were invited to attend and yet he still showed no interest. After a while, gaining John's interest became just a personal feat for Melinda. She taunted and teased him with sex, vowing to not give in to him until marriage, although she was having regular sexual relations with a paid staff member who was specifically employed for her sexual satisfaction. Unbeknownst to many, Melinda was a freak in bed and enjoyed aggressive sex.

However, the one thing Melinda wanted more than anything else was for John to genuinely want her. Every man who met her wanted her, and she wondered what made him so different. He was handsome and personable, very witty and outgoing--everything she wished she could be and everything she wanted in a man. She knew he was a well-respected new architect in her father's company and the night her father invited him to their estate she made sure she put on her best front for him to see. She knew she satisfied him visually. She knew she could satisfy him sexually but she lacked the casual dealing with lower class citizens. They were peasants to her. She didn't know how to relate to lower class citizens and didn't want to even try. She convinced herself that her father's ability to catapult John's career to heights beyond his knowledge would make him give in to her wholeheartedly. Love wasn't initially a factor for her; she just believed in winning and he was her prize. Melinda needed to ensure her family's money, power and respect would remain intact when her father could no longer run the business. She didn't know how to run the company and never aspired to do anything as such. She figured there were too many people underneath her father for her to choose from to carry on his legacy and take care of her, and John was the one she wanted. So she refused to lose the goldmine she saw in him from the first day she laid eyes on him at the company gathering months prior to his invitation to the family estate.

He was the one to ensure her family would stay wealthy and powerful. She knew John had extreme motivation and drive to bring them more independent wealth. Her father approved of their union simply because John knew the business and was a success at contractual negotiations. Matthew knew he was ill and his head-hunting mission was double pronged as he searched for a mate for his daughter as well. He was in on the scheme to land John as his son-in-law all along and he told Melinda not to mess this one up like she had destroyed the ones in the past. This time he had a plan and he suspected it would be a success. He had to get John to the altar and he knew just how he was going to do it. He was determined to secure his company's name and all the success he had grown over the years.

Melinda told her father that this relationship was different, that John actually loved her, and Matthew didn't know any different because John was trying to act as though as he was all in as well. So Matthew grew to believe John truly loved his daughter, but they were hiding one huge secret from John. Melinda was not able to bear children. Matthew knew John's stance on children. They had spoken on several occasions about how much he desired to have his own children one day. This had been a problem before with another man Melinda had dated for whom Matthew had high hopes for their future. When the discussion of children came up and Melinda revealed to him that she could not have children, he wasn't open to the option of adopting and decided to move on. He simply told her that he couldn't settle with having just the money and not his own family. So Matthew knew this could be a serious issue for John as well and didn't want to take the chance of letting him know.

However, Melinda knew why John married her from the beginning. She didn't feel that her being unable to reproduce would stop him from marrying her because he secretly enjoyed the power and the money. Instead, she was afraid that hiding her inability to have children could backfire and cause the prenuptial agreement to be null and void.

Therefore, Melinda and Matthew vowed to never let John know that they knew she was barren in the first place. The fact that Melinda held back such crucial information could cause John to win a lawsuit to dissolve the marriage and the prenuptial agreement, which could result in him owning a huge share of the company.

Melinda initially believed that within the first few years he would eventually learn to love her the way she wanted him to love her, but now, after three years of his cold and unaffectionate behavior towards her, she felt differently. Yes, they had sex hundreds of times in their marriage but Melinda could feel that his mind was always elsewhere. He would usually get intoxicated prior to them having sex. She noticed he seemed more aroused when she visited his office and they made love there but it always ended abruptly and he would jump in the shower like she made him feel dirty. Melinda wanted John to sexually satisfy her but he didn't. She rarely had orgasms and John would rarely perform oral sex on Melinda, so after a year of sexual neglect she decided to hire a fully STD-tested sexual satisfaction staff member on her personal books to take care of her sexual desires. She suspected John knew about her hired sexual fulfillment counselor and didn't even care about that because all John wanted was the money.

Melinda would never forget the day she learned about Joy. John would frequently leave for extended business trips, acquiring new contracts in different states. He had been gone for a few days when their garage door began to malfunction. Melinda suspected the batteries were dead and didn't feel like going to the store to replace them. She went to her vehicle to use the garage door opener located in the car but her car doors were locked and the keys were in the house, so she decided to use her husband's pre-programmed garage door opener in his vehicle.

As she opened the car door and reached to the center of the overhead console for the switch, a picture fell from the sun visor. It was of a young beautiful female wearing a white doctor's jacket. It had been taken in front of a pharmacy with which Melinda was familiar. It was located all the way on the other side of town. The picture looked new but was torn, as though as someone else was in the picture as well but they had been torn out completely. Melinda flipped the picture over and she recognized her husband's handwriting. He had written the name "Joy" on the back of the picture. For some reason this felt different than all his other trysts she suspected he had.

Melinda stared at the threat in the picture and thought of how much younger she was than the both of them. She had to be at least seven to ten years younger. Although she knew she was beautiful, she never felt secure in her relationship with John. She knew he just didn't love her but she still refused to let him go. Melinda thought of asking John about the picture but figured he would just lie. So she decided not to mention the picture she found just yet, but she made a duplicate of the picture and put it back above the sun visor in his car.

Melinda was always the hands-off type of woman when it came to the business but she wasn't dumb by far. She learned at a young age how to handle their money, hence the pre-nuptial agreement she and her father drew up and presented right before her wedding. Matthew taught her to always have the exact copies of all bills and accounts, including John's, that were sent to the accountant sent to the home just in case someone decided to start skimming off the top, and that's what she did. He advised her to never let John know about the personal set of documents, and she never did. Month after month, she would systematically file all the bills from each and every account they owned just in case they needed to ever conduct a personal audit.

Matthew wouldn't deem this as a reason to conduct a personal audit but Melinda definitely felt it was personal audit time. First, Melinda thoroughly searched John's car, home office, and business office but she came up with nothing. John kept separate bank accounts and credit cards and Melinda knew if there were anything to find she would find it there. She dreaded going through all those monthly statements but felt she had to know. So she spent the next two weeks combing the paperwork for more tangible evidence about Joy. Melinda rummaged through all of his clothes pockets, personal accounts and credit card bills. She didn't find much besides a monthly recurring charge for $90 on his black American Express card. The charge was made at Sheppard's Market but Melinda couldn't figure out what it could possibly be for until she found a prescription bottle along with its receipt in his inside blazer pocket. She now suspected that this was how he met Joy. *Could I be wrong? Is John sick? Did he meet her there while filling this prescription and if so, why would he have a picture of her and why would it be a secret?* Melinda wondered.

Melinda continued to dig into her husband's private life with some hope that he wasn't actually cheating. She found a number of large checks written out to a Bernard Bateman over the past three years. She wasn't familiar with a lot of the company's staff and figured it must be a contractor but made a mental note of his name. Then she discovered charges made to the six-star La'Cliffe chain of restaurants. La'Cliffe never used their true restaurant's name when placing a charge due to their confidentiality agreements, which applied both ways. However, Melinda was very familiar with the La'Cliffe chain of restaurants and businesses and also knew of the stage company names they would use lieu of their own. She thought, *How dare he take someone else to La'Cliffe! I introduced that life to him! Well, what if he had a business dinner there? I bet that's all it was!* Melinda laughed a little to herself in hopes she was correct about the business meeting even though her gut told her differently.

The next day, Melinda decided to drive herself all the way on the other side of town to visit Sheppard's Market. Everything focused around this place and she had to find out who Joy was and if she worked there. She immediately spotted the pharmacy where she suspected the woman worked.

As Melinda sat in her beautiful silver Ferrari she thought to herself, *Why am I doing this? What is the purpose? John has never loved me and now isn't any different. But I never found evidence that he was involved with another woman before. I have to find out for sure.'* Against her better judgment, Melinda got out of her car and entered the store. She perused the store like she was in search of something to buy but she really was looking for a sign of the woman in the picture. There were several associates working throughout the store but no one looked like the woman in the picture she found in her husband's car. Melinda was about to ask someone if they knew her but decided she wanted to keep this mission as stealthy as possible so asking someone about the woman was out of the question.

After purchasing a pack of gum and a magazine, Melinda decided that this was dumb and completely immature so she headed back to her car. As she exited, a young woman got out of a gold Honda Civic and approached the front door of the pharmacy wearing a white uniform lab coat. Melinda recognized her immediately from the picture and now realized that the white jacket was actually the pharmacy department's uniform. Melinda held the door purposely to get a closer look at the young woman. She was beautiful as well.

Joy smiled and spoke to her kindly and thanked her for holding the door for her. Joy continued into the pharmacy and headed to the rear of the pharmacy counter into a rear office area until she was no longer in sight. Melinda realized she was still standing in the middle of the doorway looking in Joy's direction when she was approached by another associate.

"Is everything ok, ma'am?" the young man asked her looking concerned.

Melinda was startled and quickly snapped out of her trance as she responded, "Oh yes, I just thought I forgot to get something, but I think I found everything I needed. Thank you anyway." The young man turned around and headed to a shelf that he began to stock with some new supplies as Melinda headed back to her car with the information she had come for.

All week Melinda was trying to figure out the best way to approach the subject about all the stuff she had discovered while he was away. Melinda didn't want to confront Joy and thought telling her father was a terrible idea, so she decided to handle it on her own and in her own way. She decided to just take everything day by day.

John arrived home a week later, as scheduled. Melinda was dressed in a little sexy lavender and purple lace-trimmed bustier with feather white pumps and a silk shawl to match. "So how was your business trip? Did you acquire any new contracts?" Melinda asked John, who had come into their home extra quiet after being gone for over a month on his last regional acquisition. Melinda nicely sashayed past

John so he would notice her attire and hopefully aggressively sexually attack her like he did on their honeymoon.

Instead he responded, "It was the usual. How about yours?" She knew John had to have seen what she was wearing. He had simply answered her without even looking in her direction as he headed into their personal dressing room to change.

Melinda reluctantly answered, "It was fine." The room was completely silent before Melinda stated, "I found myself on the other side of town this week at that little Sheppard's Market." She eagerly waited for his response. John paused and was quiet for a minute. He didn't really know how to respond because that was where Joy worked.

"Oh really?" John decided to say finally after a long pause. "What would take you on that side of town? Did you go alone?" John asked, not knowing if his wife had spotted him there before or not. He knew how Melinda was and figured she had to have known something to bring up Sheppard's Market out of the blue. However, he couldn't tell by her voice. She didn't sound angry so maybe she hadn't.

She finally responded, "Unfortunately, there is this face cream my grandmother used that is awesome. I checked all over this town and it just so happens that the only place that carries it around here is that little raggedy market. Isn't it something dear that a little shabby pharmacy on the other side of town has something I need in it? Isn't that just crazy?"

John still wasn't sure if Melinda was on to his antics with Joy or not, but he continued on with the charade and said, "Yes, that is crazy."

"You are familiar with the store I'm talking about, aren't you, John?" Melinda asked.

John felt it was a trick question but stuck with his plan to play completely dumb about the matter. "Well, yeah, sort of. It's been a while since I've been there, though."

At that instant, Melinda wanted to walk into their dressing room and smash his face into the mirror and clear through the wall to the drywall studs. Luckily, he couldn't see the rage in her face from where he stood purposely trying to avoid her in the dressing room. Melinda had reviewed all of his credit card statements and all of his personal accounts that she was aware of and knew without a doubt that John was lying.

Melinda was pissed but didn't want him to know how much she knew just yet. Nothing else seemed out of place in their lives and she didn't want to jump the gun. But he had already lied about being at the pharmacy, so what else was he hiding, she wondered.

"Hey John. Some man called the house for you the other day."

"Some man?" John asked. "Well, who was it?"

Melinda hesitated before answering, then stated, "I think he said Don... ummm, Bernard something. Oh yeah, it was Bernard Bateman."

John's head snapped to attention and he swung around to face Melinda. "What do you mean?" he asked her.

"What do you mean, what do I mean? Someone called here looking for you," Melinda lied again.

"Well, did he say anything else?"

"No, he only asked for you and I said you weren't home. Who is he, John?""No one important," John answered, then he walked out of the bedroom to avoid any more inquisition from Melinda. John thought, *What the hell was that about? Did someone really call or does Melinda know something? I have to make sure there are no loose ends before my whole plan blows up in my face.*

Melinda watched as John walked out of the bedroom and figured he just didn't want to talk anymore. Melinda headed downstairs toward the kitchen. John peeked down the stairs to see if she was really gone as he walked to his closet to open a hidden wall safe he had installed when Melinda wasn't home. He retrieved a brown briefcase from inside and deposited a number of blank company checks, new photographs of Joy and a prescription bottle. He kept most of his personal things that he didn't want her to know about at his little apartment but he also kept a few items in this safe. It hadn't appeared to have been tampered with so he couldn't understand why she brought up Bernard Bateman or Sheppard's Market.

He finished making his usual deposits of the personal effects he kept of Joy throughout the week. John enjoyed photographing Joy in public. He had accumulated hundreds of random pictures he had taken of her at work, her college and various places around town. As John looked at one of the photos he had taken of Joy with Sophie at the playground, he chuckled and thought, *She would think I'm a stalker if she ever saw these.* John then looked at the prescription bottles and counted them. He quickly realized he was short one and panicked until he remembered it was in the inside pocket of a blazer he rarely wore. He went back into the dressing room to retrieve the bottle from the blazer he had worn one evening with Joy. John thought, *Whew, good thing Melinda didn't see these because she would have known I been to the market after all, and I don't want her causing trouble for Joy.* Then he dropped them into the briefcase and locked it back. *I'm going to take these pills back to the office with me so I can flush them all down the toilet without her sneaking up on me. Yeah, I'll do that. Then I have to find out what she meant about Bernard calling. Is someone setting me up?* John thought as he put the small briefcase into the larger one to discreetly take it out of the house.

Chapter 11 - Looking a Little Deeper

MELINDA WALKED INTO her study and looked at the pile of mail she failed to put away after her personal audit of all the bills. She rolled her eyes at the stack of papers then picked up the phone to make a call she was hoping she wouldn't have to make. "Hello, I would like to hire a private investigator. I believe my husband is having an affair and I would like to know every little detail about a woman named Joy. I don't know her last name yet, but I'm sure your services would close that gap as well. She works at the pharmacy in that little shabby Sheppard's Market. That's all the information I have as of yet. I expect you will provide me with much more soon."

"Yes ma'am, we could provide twenty-four hour services to you if you like," the man stated with a Southern drawl.

"That would be perfect. When can you start?"

"Well ma'am, I can get started on the case today, after we sign a contract and set up the initial payment."

"Okay, well start now. I'm Melinda Mack-Conglin and I assure you I will be able to satisfy whatever fee you invoice. I would like updates every six hours of her whereabouts and anyone who is accompanying her as well, and speak to no one about this besides me. Understood?"

"Ahh, did you say Conglin as in the Conglins from ADC?"

"Yes, exactly."

"Well, yes!" Wilbur said excitedly. "I understand you want to start right away, but ma'am, I really wish you would go through the company-required paperwork first. I mean, you don't even know MY name."

"What is your name?" Melinda rudely snapped at the man.

"Wilbur. My name is Wilbur Wright. My mother and father started this company...."

"Okay, okay, okay, Wil-bur," Melinda rudely cut him off again. "Honestly, I really don't really care what your name is. I have your company's name; therefore, I can get the information I need whenever I need it. However, since you're so concerned about making this a personal deal, I'll hold you responsible for the investigation. Now get started. I'll hear from you in six hours."

Melinda hung up the phone and looked at her watch, longing for six hours to pass to have her first piece of information about Joy.

Wilbur sat at his little dusty desk, thrilled to finally get a case after a major dry spell with the business. *But why would she choose my little company?* he thought. He immediately ran a check on Melinda Conglin. *Wow, she's like a baby Hilton. That's why she wanted to use a small company. She doesn't want anyone to find out about this.*

"Well, baby Hilton, I'm going to drag this investigation out so long that I'm not going to have to work for the next five years and with your nasty attitude I won't even feel bad about doing it this time either." He quickly gathered his things and headed to Sheppard's Market to learn more about Joy.

It didn't take long for Wilbur to find out all he needed to know about Joy. In less than a week he had discovered that Joy wasn't the problem at all. It was the man stalking her every move and taking pictures of her in public places. Wilbur identified the man as Melinda's husband, John. Wilbur watched as John would park near Joy's home and observe another man visit her from time to time. The other man's vehicle had out-of-state tags and resembled John's. Wilbur noted the registration and found the vehicle listed to a Mr. Dwight Moss of Newcomb. Wilbur also witnessed John, Joy and Dwight conversing a few times like old friends. Wilbur was convinced that Joy and John didn't have a sexual relationship but since he needed money, he would string Melinda along for a little while longer. He decided to give Melinda what she was looking for after he followed John and Joy to a restaurant on the opposite side of town then called Melinda to come witness it for herself.

Wilbur called Melinda to meet him at 7th and Waycross Avenue. Melinda pulled up behind his black Suburban. Wilbur motioned for her to get inside his truck. He couldn't wait to get a glance at the woman he had been conversing with every six hours for the past three days. Melinda slowly exited her car. Wilbur watched as her shapely left leg slowly exited the door first. She wore ultra-sheer stockings and three and a half inch spectator pumps. Her coat dress was a tangerine color with black buttons that were buttoned down to reveal a good portion of her cleavage. Her hair was long brown and flowed around her vanilla-colored skin. Her lipstick matched her dress and her eyes were perfectly dressed from the brows to the lashes. She clutched a spectator purse that matched her shoes as she sashayed to the passenger side of the truck. Wilbur watched as she stood outside the door looking into the window. Wilbur rolled down the passenger side window and said, "It's open."

"Excuse me? Do you expect me to open my own door?"

"Sure, unless you want to climb through the window," he chuckled.

Melinda rolled her eyes as she lifted the door handle and hoisted herself into the big truck. "This better be worth all this, Mr. Wright," she stated as she smoothed down her dress and crossed her ankles in the truck."

Wilbur pointed to a little restaurant across the street from an industrial park. "Do you see what I see?" he asked her.

"Look, I don't pay you to play games, Mr. Wright!"

"You haven't actually paid me anything yet, so I guess you're right about that." He chuckled again.

Melinda glared at Wilbur then stated, "Paying you is not a problem!"

Wilbur shook his head and said, "You're a spoiled little cute thing, aren't you? Just got to have your way. I can see that already. All cute and pouty for no darn reason. Well, I'm not worried about you paying me cause I'm sure you don't want the fact that your husband is right over there, in that-there restaurant, with that-there woman, to get out to the public. I just wanted you to come on out here and see it for yourself."

"Look, Wil-bur, you work for me..."

"Oh please! Woman, stop with the bossy 'you work for me' shenanigans! I actually work for MYSELF and just chose to take on YOUR case. I don't give a hill of beans who your daddy is, or how much money y'all got. I'm here to do a job and that's what I'm going to do and you're gonna allow me to do it MY way, starting with signing this-here agreement for services rendered already and in the future."

Melinda and Wilbur were in a dead stare at one another as he handed her the contract to sign. "Go on ahead now, you're wasting precious time."

Melinda was speechless. She wasn't used to someone discounting her self-proclaimed authority. Melinda turned her head and ignored the contract as she gazed out the window toward the restaurant. She imagined Joy and John inside cuddled up together, laughing like the happy little couple.

"Ummm, Melinda, can you sign the contract, please?"

"Fuck the contract; I said I will take care of whatever you invoice me!" Melinda yelled then jumped out of the truck, slammed the door and headed toward the restaurant.

"Is that really how a lady speaks? Spoiled ass!"

Wilbur laughed and shook his head as he watched Melinda walk across the street like a spoiled brat. "Why do I have that woman thinking that man is having an affair? I'm not even going to tell her about Dwight Moss; she can learn about that on her own," Wilbur said to himself as he continued to watch Melinda stomp across the street toward the restaurant.

Chapter 12 - Ohhh Noooo!

JOY HAD BEEN running from her classes to the library and to work for months, trying to complete several assignments in between working long hours and taking care of Sophie. Her relationship with Dwight was hot and heavy whenever he came to town. He had her car repaired for her and she was thankful for the assistance. She couldn't afford to get it fixed on her own and refused John's help to pay for the repairs. She tried to pick up additional hours at work but found that her grades always began to slip when she did. It was imperative that she stayed at the top of her classes so she could easily slide into the graduate medical PharmD program she so desired. Everything was going well until Susan came home from work one day and found Joy slumped over the toilet barfing her brains out.

"Are you okay?" Susan asked. Joy kept coughing, gagging and vomiting a thick yellowish substance. She had been extremely tired the past week but pushed herself to the limit, at times even going without eating anything all day, so she didn't think anything of it. Joy finally stopped vomiting and slowly stood up from the toilet. The pungent smell of vomit filled the bathroom and Joy had an embarrassed look on her face. Susan grabbed a facecloth and wet it to help Joy wipe her face and mouth. Joy's eyes were dark and swollen underneath and the inside was red.

"Are you okay?" Susan asked again.

"Yes, I've just been doing too much lately. It's finals time and it seems like I don't have any energy to do anything these days," Joy answered meekly.

"How about you take the day off from work and just lie down and rest? I'll watch Sophie. I don't know why you push yourself so hard, Joy. You know Patrick and I would help you with whatever you need," Susan said while shuffling Joy to the bedroom to lie down.

"I know, Susan; I'm just not comfortable with that. It's bad enough that I stay with you guys rent free. Both of you are helping me more than enough now," Joy said sadly.

"Look at it this way, Joy; this is our way of extending the blessings God has given us all these years. This is nothing to us. An extra vacant room in a condo that's completely empty more than half of the time is nothing, Joy. Please take it easy; your brother would want that," Susan said as she closed Joy's blinds and left the room.

Joy fell sound asleep until she felt an urge to jump up and run to the bathroom to vomit again. As she was puking the yellowish substance again she smelled a horrific odor emanating from the kitchen. Susan heard Joy in the bathroom again and went to check on her.

"You must have a stomach bug, Joy. I was in there fixing your favorite for lunch but I don't know if you can eat anything for a while the way you're vomiting today."

Joy looked at Susan with a twisted look in her face and asked, "What is that smell?" Susan looked surprised. Joy had always loved Susan's homemade lasagna and could smell it from a mile away. But this time the smell was nauseating to Joy.

"It's lasagna. I thought it was your favorite. I was trying to make you feel better. I don't know why you don't like the smell. I didn't put anything different in it." Susan looked concerned and perplexed at Joy. Joy apologized. She could tell Susan was greatly offended by her question.

"I'm sorry, Susan; you must be right. I just have a stomach bug or something." Joy began to wash her face and brush her teeth again. This time she called her job to tell them she wouldn't be at work. They told her to rest and to not worry about the day. Joy went back into her room and, since she was awake, decided to try to get a little studying done. She reviewed her class schedule and calendar for the upcoming assignments when she realized the red circle around the 5th of the month. She jumped up and ran to her wall calendar to check the date again, which was circled in red as well. The room began to spin as she stared at the calendar, trying to think back to her last menstrual cycle. It had been over a month ago.

"Oh my God," she stated. "It can't be!" She quickly ran to the wall calendar and looked at the date and it displayed the 29th. "Oh my God! That's almost four weeks late! How did I miss my period?" She frantically grabbed her head. "This can't be right!"

Joy pulled out every planner book and calendar she owned, only to find the same date circled indicating her menstrual cycle's due date. She was always so meticulous when it came to scheduling. However, she knew she had been careless a few times and hadn't used protection when she and Dwight made love. She walked over to the old Victorian style mirror that was hanging over her long dresser beside Sophie's bed. She stared at herself in disgust and disappointment as a tear dropped down her face. Joy then asked herself, "What am I going to do now?"

Chapter 13 - Face the Music

DWIGHT HAD NOT been to town for the majority of the month and Joy was thrilled, because she wasn't in the mood to face him about the possible baby she was carrying just yet. Joy normally called him often, and she knew he was probably wondering what was going on with her. She felt she never knew which one of Dwight's personalities she would get, so she wanted to make sure she knew what she wanted to do before she revealed anything to him. She loved Dwight and believed he loved her but one minute he would be nice and sweet and the next he would be short and crass. They had discussed his nasty demeanor toward her several times and he equated it to stress with his company and left it at that. Overall, Joy still enjoyed being around him and found herself in a deep, volatile, long distance relationship with him.

Recently, whenever Dwight called, she would make up an excuse to get off of the phone. Dwight never made a big deal about her not speaking with him like before, and that really bothered her. She wanted him to care and to force the issue to talk and see her but he didn't. Although she felt she needed time to figure out what she wanted to do about the baby, she still wanted him to act like he cared even a little about her recent change in demeanor. This was simply an example of some things about Dwight that she didn't like. He seemed so self-consumed that nothing in her life was important. And she often asked herself if she wanted to spend the rest of her life that way.

Joy had also put her friendship with John on the back burner. He had called her often but she would always end the call abruptly. Then Shay informed her he had even stopped by the pharmacy a few times, only to discover she hadn't been to work all week. John felt something was wrong and thought it had something to do with Melinda since she had mentioned Sheppard's Market, but he wasn't for certain. John knew Joy would never miss her classes so he drove to the college and waited for her to come out, like he did often, just to photograph her and see her face.

Just like clockwork Joy exited the Magnolia Hall from her pharmaceutical sciences class and headed in the direction of the library.

There's my baby, John thought. John stepped out of the car and walked over to her. "Hello beautiful," he said softly.

Joy immediately recognized the voice and swung around to see John standing there smiling. She looked from side to side and then asked, "What are you doing here?"

John took her books out her hand and said, "Taking you to lunch, of course." Then he left her standing there and started walking toward his car. Joy stood in the same spot in awe at his audacity in showing up at her college uninvited and basically demanding that she to go to lunch. Joy watched as John continued to walk without turning around once to see if she was following. John knew she would follow him. He thought, *What choice does she have? I took her books.*

Joy reluctantly followed John to his car and silently slid into the soft, pale yellow leather seats. She looked around the inside of his vehicle, not realizing why she hadn't noticed the similarity of John and Dwight's vehicles before. She sat silently as John drove to a cozy little Italian restaurant on the outskirts of town. John parked the car and walked to the passenger side to open the door for Joy but she had already started opening her car door and jumped out before he could reach the handle. She grabbed her purse and walked ahead of him into the restaurant without saying a word. John knew something was really wrong and prayed he could fix the situation. He thought, *I hope she didn't find out about Melinda, my obsession for her or about Bernard. I've been discreet; I don't see how she would know.*

John had the hostess seat them in a secluded booth to the rear of the restaurant. Joy excused herself to go to the restroom. Unbeknownst to John, she was vomiting as usual like she did all day nowadays. When she returned to the table, John stood up until she sat.

"What would you like to drink?" a young female waiter asked them both.

"I'll take a hot tea," said Joy. John looked up from his menu at Joy, who looked back at him. They stared at each other eye to eye before Joy broke the stare and looked down at her menu. Her eyes were swollen, red and puffy and her voice was raspy. He smiled at her and turned to the waitress and said, "Yes, make that two hot teas, two chicken noodle soups and lots of oyster crackers." Joy looked up from her menu at John. He smiled at her again and said, "So, is he happy?" Joy turned her head to look out the window beside her booth. "Hello. Earth to Joyyy," John said jokingly. "Woman, you really had me worried. I'm used to hearing from you at least twice a week and there you go M.I.A. for a week." John was trying his best to make her smile, but nothing seemed to work. Joy was still silent and looking towards the greenery on the other side of the street. Finally, John said, "Do I have to contact Dwight to find out what's going on with you? You know he would absolutely love that," he smirked.

Joy's head snapped toward John as she said, "Don't you dare contact Dwight!"

John retorted, "Well, if you don't talk to me, what choice do I have?" John knew he had no intention of contacting Dwight and had pretty much figured out what was wrong with Joy already.

"Look John, I think I'm pregnant," Joy finally said as the waitress walked up again to bring their hot teas.

"Okay," John said. "What's the big deal? I'm happy if you're happy. I thought everything was fine between you and ole lover-boy, Dwight. Isn't he happy about the baby?"

Every time John referred to Dwight as a lover-boy it bugged Joy. "He's not a lover-boy, John. And I haven't even confirmed it yet, so I haven't told him anything."

"Well, it's not hard to tell with the puffy, red eyes and bad attitude," John said as he laughed at her cuteness to him. Joy didn't laugh at all. John stopped joking around and said, "Look, I don't know what's going on with you and Dwight, but it's best that you go ahead and take the test and if you are pregnant, tell him the truth as soon as possible. That's all you can do. I'm sure he will stand by your side. You guys have been dating almost a year. Why wouldn't he?"

Joy looked at John with soft, teary eyes and silently wished it was this easy to talk to Dwight, but it wasn't and this subject would be even harder. "You're right. I will call him and let him know tonight, right after I pick up a pregnancy test," Joy said with a faint smile on her face.

As Joy and John continued their conversation and sipped on their bowls of soup, they didn't notice they were being watched. Wilbur had been tailing Joy all day and as soon as John met up with her at the college, he knew he was about to make his big bucks.

Chapter 14 - Mislead

MELINDA WALKED INTO the restaurant after being tipped off by Wilbur. The same hostess that seated Joy and John seated Melinda. As the waitress walked past she summoned her to have a seat. "How would you like to receive an extra-large tip today, young lady?" Melinda asked the waitress. The tone in which Melinda spoke was of some type of authority and instantly the waitress surmised that she had something to offer.

The young waitress looked at Melinda from head to toe. She noticed her expensive shoes first, then her watch and other jewelry. She thought, *Who walks around this part of town wearing real three carat diamond studs in their freaking ears?* She finally answered Melinda's question sarcastically, "I like to get them every day and it depends on what you mean by extra large and what I have to do to get it."

"All I need, young lady, is some information on what that couple over there in the last booth is talking about."

The waitress turned around to where Melinda discreetly pointed and thought, *Ummmm, she's all dressed up and her man's out here creeping. I shouldn't help this chick get nothing! Should make her go over there herself.* The waitress wasn't going to lose out on a money making opportunity, though. She turned back to face Melinda and asked, "What are you offering for that type of information because that will be at least a hundred dollars."

Melinda smirked at the young lady and stated, "One hundred--is that all? That's a deal. How about you go over there now so you can provide that information to me pronto, and it will be worth four hundred more cash dollars for you."

Melinda eyeballed the young waitress as she got excited and stated, "Yeah, right--are you kidding me?"

Melinda pulled out her authentic Louis Vuitton wallet full of crisp hundred dollar bills. She handed the waitress a one hundred dollar bill and stated, "This is my retainer."

"Well shit, that is easy! I don't have to go over there to tell you that. I can tell you right now what they are talking about. I heard the whole story already and you can give me all my money," the waitress stated to Melinda while staring at her loaded wallet.

"Ok. So what are they talking about?" Melinda handed the young lady another one hundred dollar bill.

"You said five hundred but Imma trust you gonna be a woman of your word after I tell you this. Anyway, the chick is pregnant with the dude's baby and I heard him say something about what's the big deal and that he was happy." The waitress expected Melinda to run over to the table and for all hell to break loose. She actually wanted to see the drama unfold and couldn't believe she just made $500 off snitching on an affair. However, Melinda didn't say another word. She simply handed the waitress the three hundred she owed her, got up gracefully and walked out of the restaurant. The waitress placed her hands on her hips, shook her head and stated to herself, *Couldn't have been me--A BABY TOO!*

Boogie Bitches, I tell ya, I woulda been whooping somebody's ass in here today! The waitress cleared her table and went back to work, happy about the $500 she had just made.

Melinda headed back to her car with obvious fury on her face. Wilbur watched as she jumped in her Ferrari and slammed the door. Wilbur quickly jumped out of his truck and headed to her car. "Excuse me, Melinda, but I really need you to go ahead and sign this if you want me to continue my services." Wilbur motioned to hand Melinda the contract through her rolled up driver's side window. Melinda rolled down her window without saying a word then snatched the paper from Wilbur. Wilbur smiled as she signed the papers without reading the ten thousand dollar retainer, along with the recurring five thousand dollar monthly payments to be made until a written request to discontinue payment was received. She swiftly handed the papers back to Wilbur, turned her head back to the front of the windshield, started her car and started rolling up the driver's side window. "Excuse me, Melinda, but where should I submit the invoice?"

"Send them to my accountant," she said through the closed window.

"Well, ummm, what's the accountant's contact information?"

Melinda rolled her window back down and glared at Wilbur before she stated, "You're the damn investigator! Figure it out!" Then she stepped on the gas and sped off toward the highway.

Wilbur took off his dirty old denim baseball cap and scratched his head. He watched as Melinda sped out of sight and shook his head as he stated, "Somebody ruined you, gull. You're just too darn pretty to be such an asshole." He continued to shake his head as he headed back to his car.

Joy left the restaurant after an hour with John, feeling happy and refreshed. She no longer felt her life and future were over because of her possible pregnancy, and she thought that was all because of John's sincere guidance about her ordeal. John had come through again for her. He successfully convinced her to talk to Dwight, and that's exactly what she was going to do.

John stopped at a nearby market and found a little drugstore to purchase Joy two pregnancy tests. Then he dropped her off at her brother's condo. But John didn't realize he was being followed. Wilbur tailed them all the way from the restaurant to the drugstore, where he photographed John through the window as he purchased pregnancy tests for Joy. Then he followed them back to Joy's place and photographed Joy as she gave John a big hug and kiss on his cheek. Wilbur conducted his six hour check-in with Melinda and told her of the photographs he had taken after their lunch date. Melinda was already heading to John's office to wait for his return. She was ready to get down to the bottom of this Joy issue once and for all.

Chapter 15 - Facing the Truth

"HELLOOOO. IS ANYBODY HOME?" Joy yelled through the condo. *Good. I'm here alone,* she thought as she scrambled to her bedroom and opened the bag containing the pregnancy tests. She went into the bathroom and ran a hot lavender and chamomile bubble bath. As she watched the tub fill with water she stopped, leaned over the bathroom sink and dropped her head as she began to pray. "Lord, I know I haven't always come to you for guidance and I know I can do much better by you in my life, but please Lord, if I am pregnant please, please, please help me along this journey. If I appeared to never need you Lord, I confess, I need you now! Amen." Joy raised her head as she looked at her reflection in the mirror.

"Okay girl," she said to herself. "Let's do this." Joy opened the package and read the instructions. "So all I have to do is pee on this stick and if I see a plus sign I'm pregnant." Joy sat on the toilet and placed the little white stick beneath her as she started to urinate. *Ughhhh. This sucks!* she thought as she closed her eyes and pulled the stick from underneath her. She counted to ten before she opened her eyes, only to see a definite plus sign in the window of the test strip. Joy dropped the test strip on the floor and held her head in her hands for over ten minutes.

The phone started ringing in the other room. It had rung three times since she had been home but she refused to answer it for fear it might be Dwight.

Joy ignored the phone again as she cut the bathroom lights off, opened the bathroom window and closed the curtains to only allow a minimum amount of light to shine through. She took her clothes off then slowly sank into the lukewarm bubble bath she had prepared just for this moment. There was a fresh breeze blowing through the window. The relaxing smell of lavender and chamomile filled the bathroom and provided the perfect atmosphere for Joy to clear her mind.

She looked down at her perfectly flat stomach and began to rub it, imagining it fat and round. She began to smile at the thought of carrying a baby inside her once again and hoped Dwight would be thrilled. She recalled him joking about her as being the one for him but it was never anything definite. He would always change the subject before it got too deep. She just knew he would marry her one day but now it needed to be a little bit sooner. Then Joy thought of the issues she had with Dwight's selfishness but thought this had to be different since it was about his own child. Then Joy thought about her brother and all he and Susan had done for her and Sophie. The thought of having to tell them made her sad. She never wanted to disappoint them. Joy sat up in the tub as she thought, *One thing at a time and the first thing on my list is telling Dwight.* Joy got out the tub and put on her robe as she headed to the phone and dialed Dwight's number.

"Joy! I've been calling you for days! Where have you been?"

"Around," she answered dryly.

"Around? What kind of answer is that? If I could have cancelled some of these investment meetings, I would have come there to make sure you were okay. I was on my way tomorrow, though. Why are you avoiding my calls? Did I do something wrong?"

Joy sat quietly on the phone for a few seconds. She could hear Dwight breathing in the phone and knew he was anxiously awaiting her answer.

Joy finally said, "I've been sick all week."

"Sick? What, you catch the flu or something?"

"No. I'm pregnant."

"PREGNANT! What do you mean you're pregnant! I thought you were on the pill!"

Joy remained silent on the phone.

"We don't even do it that much, Joy! I'm out of town most of the time! I don't understand! You're on the pill and I use condoms sometimes! What the hell! And the two times we didn't use a condom I pulled out! A baby! That would interfere with my business plans right now. This just isn't a good time! And how is my family going to take it knowing I got some girl pregnant that they haven't even met yet! This is so messed up!"

Dwight went on and on and Joy never felt as low as she felt at that moment.

"Oh now I'm just 'some girl.' And who gives a fuck what your family thinks, Dwight! This isn't just about you! But of course you think it is, like every damn thing else is alllll about you!"

"What do you mean?"

"Well, you say this isn't a 'good time.' Apparently you HAD a good time when you made this baby inside me!" Tears began to run down her face as she could hear Dwight saying something between her words but couldn't make out what he said.

"I can't believe you would treat me like this! You're just like all the rest of these sorry-ass men who get what they want and run off when it's time to step up to the plate. I thought you were different! Goodbye, asshole!"

Joy slammed the phone down as hard as she could. She was shaking and crying when she felt a hand touch her shoulder. She swung around and saw her brother and Susan standing there. Susan reached out and hugged Joy as her brother said, "Don't worry. Everything will be okay for you, Sophie and the baby. We will make sure of that."

Chapter 16 - The Confrontation

MELINDA RARELY VISITED the office but was always welcomed by the highly paid staff. She tried her best to keep a smile on her face as she passed the many offices and cubicles on the way to her husband's corner office. She wanted to cry from the pain she felt inside after what she had just seen with her own eyes. She couldn't believe what she had just discovered about her husband and Joy. The fact that Melinda couldn't have children of her own made it even worse.

Melinda slowly opened the opaque glass office door and looked around the office they had designed together only a few years ago. From the soft Italian leather love seat to the posh plush carpeting contouring the seating area of his office, everything was handpicked, imported and customized just to his liking. She thought of how excited John was when her father appointed him as CEO of their region and awarded him with this office and many more royalties. She remembered them making love on the desk, chair, table, ottoman, window sill and floor. In her mind she knew things would never be perfect but it was okay. She blushed as she remembered getting a little too loud one or two times. She knew some of his little employees wanted to be more than just employees so she had to mark her territory every once and awhile. But marking her territory wasn't the purpose of her visit that day. Her purpose that day was keeping what was hers.

Melinda sat at John's desk and cut on the television, patiently waiting for his return. Two hours had passed and according to John's secretary, his meeting was scheduled to be over an hour ago. But Melinda knew he wasn't at a meeting at all, just like he probably wasn't out of town on meetings or contractual acquisitions. She figured he was with this Joy person all this time. Melinda headed to the private restroom in the office and noticed a brown briefcase she had never seen before on the top of a shelf. She retrieved the briefcase and took it back to the desk. Right as she was opening the briefcase John walked into the office. She looked down into the briefcase and there were pictures of Joy. She gasped as John rushed over to grab the briefcase from her.

"What the hell are you doing going through my things in my office!" John shouted.

"No, what the hell have you been doing, John?!" Tears began to fall down her face. She dropped the multiple pictures she was holding of Joy and watched as they fluttered about the office floor. There were hundreds of pictures of Joy in the briefcase--some of her carrying books smiling, some at the supermarket, some in a club and even some in the passenger side of his car, among many others.

Melinda tearfully opened her tangerine button-down coat-dress and exposed her brand new black and white lacey lingerie. Her body and legs were like silk, her makeup was perfect and lips were luscious, but her eyes were red and full of tears and her forehead was wrinkled with disgust.

"I guess you don't want this anymore?" she stated as she touched her breasts and motioned toward her vagina. "Every other man on the planet does, but this isn't good enough for you! It never has been!" she yelled. "You never wanted me to be your wife, but you wanted my family's money and power, didn't you, so that's why your greedy, poor, good for nothing ass married me!"

John picked up the briefcase and put all the pictures back inside. He also quickly retrieved several blank checks, prescription bottles and a set of extra keys to his secret apartment.

"What the hell are those?!" she asked, pointing to the keys, not even noticing the blank checks. "Are those the keys to that bitch's place?"

John closed the briefcase and turned to his wife and said, "How about you learn to have some class, put on some clothes, and stop thinking your sex appeal will get you anything you want? And apparently I am good for something, because if I weren't you wouldn't still want me. I'll see you when I get home." Then he walked out of the office and left Melinda standing and crying, all alone and half naked in her lingerie.

As John left his office, he thought about how Melinda had badgered him for years about having affairs, although he had never had one. The only affair he would have considered having would have been with Joy. He shook his head as he recalled Melinda looking at Joy's pictures as they fell to the floor. At least she doesn't know who Joy is, he thought. How am I going to explain all those pictures? Joy doesn't even know I took them. I just wanted to see her in every facet of her life.

Then John thought about Dwight. He was really afraid that Joy would end up marrying Dwight and was thrilled when Dwight acted as though as he did not want the baby.

John knew Joy was head over heels about Dwight. He was handsome, intelligent and had his own company as well. He could take care of Joy the way John wanted to and most of all, she was in love with him. She always spoke highly of him and jumped to his defense all the time. John envied Dwight's relationship with Joy and always thought he was taking Joy for granted. John felt Dwight could have made himself more available when Joy needed him. Instead, Joy constantly complained to John about the way Dwight only seemed to see her when he wanted to and he never put her priorities first. However, Joy was loyal to him and would not break off the relationship, even though John had suggested it several times. John knew Joy's love for Dwight was a threat to him having a future with her. But after today, John wouldn't have to worry about Dwight as much anymore.

John arrived home hours later, after leaving Melinda standing in his office angry and crying. It was late and the house was dark. The only light visible was coming from the pool through the morning room windows where Melinda stood dressed in the same sexy lingerie she wore in his office earlier that day. Her presence startled John, so he quickly flicked on the light. Melinda stood motionless, holding an empty glass. Her makeup was no longer flawless. The mascara and eyeliner had smeared above and beneath her eyes. Her lipstick was completely gone from her lips and her hair was down, tangled and messy. She was facing John but was standing so still that she could have been mistaken for a mannequin in a department store. The look of her gave John the chills. He shook his head and continued to walk to the double staircase.

"So you're just going to keep going like nothing happened today?" she muttered. John didn't respond. "Did you actually think I wouldn't find out?" John continued walking but could now hear Melinda slowly following him. "How long, John?" John kept walking. "HOW LONG?!" she yelled. John kept walking quietly ignoring her questions. "Well, I knew about her a long time ago. I've been watching your sneaky ass! You're not the only one who has pictures, John! I have pictures too! I'm sure my attorneys will have a field day with them!" She followed him quietly down the hall and up the back staircase to his office. "How long have you been seeing this Joy person, John?" she asked calmly this time.

John placed his briefcase down on the desk and wondered how Melinda knew Joy's name. He took off his suit jacket and swung it around his chair. He never faced Melinda and continued to ignore her questions.

"ANSWER ME! YOU CHEATING BASTARD! You never answer my questions! You hear me talking to you!"

John finally turned around calmly and looked at Melinda and said, "Look at yourself. You're pathetic. I want out of this marriage as of yesterday, and I want my portion of the business. I'm leaving and I'll get the rest of my stuff later." John walked in their bedroom and packed an overnight bag then walked to the garage to get his car.

Melinda followed him all the way to the garage. "Leaving! Leaving! And where the hell do you think you're going?!"

John continued to ignore Melinda as he threw his overnight bag into the trunk of his black Mercedes Benz, jumped into his car and sped off into the night.

Chapter 17 – Silence Isn't So Bliss

"DAMN, DAMN, DAMN!" Dwight screamed as he slammed the phone several times against its receiver before placing it down.

"Hey dude, if you break it you own it. What's wrong with you?" Dwight's brother Dwayne asked as he passed through the office.

"Joy just hung up on me and now she won't take my calls."

"Oh, that's it. She'll get over whatever it is in a little while, I'm sure. Women always do that," Dwayne said confidently.

"No, she won't and I'm not either! I wish I wasn't out of town. I need to see her right away."

"What's going on? Who is this Joy, anyway? Is this a serious relationship? I've never known you to be in a serious relationship." Dwayne chuckled at the thought.

"Yeah man, and you have to promise me you won't tell the family anything if I decide to tell you what's going on."

"Okay man. You know me better than that. Come on now. I wouldn't say anything to anybody. But this must be serious for real. So talk to me."

"All right, meet me at the spot later, around three o'clock, because I have to go out of town later to catch up with her. Plus, I got something important I need to do before I see her."

"All right, I'll be there. See you later."

Later that day, Dwight parked his car at Cantucci's but didn't see his brother anywhere in sight. He walked in and received all the normal greetings from the regulars that visited the upscale bar. "Where have you been hiding, handsome?" a young waitress named Carla asked.

Dwight looked at the young lady, who was fairly attractive but nowhere near the caliber of his Joy, physically or mentally. Dwight gave her a nice smile and answered, "I've been out of town on business."

"Well, you definitely should take me next time. I can be your personal assistant."

"Definitely not, no offense." Dwight walked away and headed to his private seating area on the landing above the entrance, where he could see almost the entire bar area below.

"Would you like your usual, Mr. Moss?" another young waitress asked.

"Yes. Please. Tiffany, make it a double." She just smiled, nodded her head and headed to the bar to make his all-too-usual Grand Mariner on the rocks. Dwight finally observed Dwayne walk into the establishment. Carla pulled her same classic moves on Dwayne. She flirted with him like all the men who walked through the door. Dwayne flirted back with her then headed up the staircase to meet Dwight.

Dwight stood up as his brother approached. "Hey man, what took you so long?"

They fist bumped and Dwayne responded, "I was busy doing what you need to do more often!" They both laughed.

"Naw man, I'm getting all mine and some. As a matter of fact that's why I called you here today."

"Man, you better not have knocked up Carla. She's fine as hell and phat as shit, but I heard she burned a couple of these dudes in here."

Dwight shook his head and waved his hands. "Naw bruh! I wouldn't touch that with my worst enemy's dick!"

Dwayne laughed, "Well, I'll tap that with two condoms, some Nonoxynol 9, and some Lysol."

"I bet you would! I think she thought you were me, Dwayne."

"Yeah, she probably did. But that's nothing new, everybody does. So what's up? Why did you rush me over here today and why were you so stressed out earlier?

"I did something major today. And I need your blessing because I haven't talked to anybody else in the family about this." Dwight reached in his pocket and pulled out a small black bag. "Dwayne, I don't know if I messed up, but I'm going to try to fix things tonight. I'm in love and I'm going to be a father."

"What!" Dwayne exclaimed. "Who! When! How!"

"I think you know HOW! I just can't believe I'm going to be a father! This is the happiest day of my life! Look what I bought her today." He opened the little black bag and revealed a black velvet jewelry case. "I have to make my baby legitimate." Dwight opened the jewelry case and revealed a platinum and gold diamond engagement ring. "You think she will like it?"

Dwayne looked at the three-carat, solitaire princess-cut stone, set in a platinum finish and surrounded by mini-princess cut stones to encircle the remainder of the band. "If she doesn't like it bring it to me; I'll marry your punk ass!" Both men laughed and took down one of several shots they ordered from the waitress.

"I love this girl, Wayne. I really do. She is beautiful and smart and I just want to do right by her and our baby. She is so sweet. She never asked for anything. She puts up with all my shit all the time. I haven't even introduced her to the family yet. I guess I'll set up a dinner for this week and that's where I'll tell them all about us. She has been so stressed out with classes and work recently. I'm sure this will bring a smile to her face."

"Ok man, I hear you. But why do you think you messed up? I don't understand."

"I sort of panicked when she told me about the baby. I said a lot of things that didn't exactly come out right at the time and she took it the wrong way. I just got to let her know I'm going to do right by her and my baby. She wouldn't let me get a word in after I realized what I had said. I feel awful. But I'm going to fix it tonight!"

"If she is the one for you, go for it," Dwayne said while patting Dwight on his shoulder.

Dwight hugged his brother and told him, "Well, let me get out of here. I have to get on the road before rush hour traffic to make it to Juniper at a reasonable hour. I haven't talked to her since she called me about the baby earlier today."

"Juniper?" Dwayne repeated. "Oh, she lives out there where the new office is supposed to be."

"Yeah, but she thinks it's up and running already. I haven't told her much about the family or the business. I was trying to get myself together first. You know, get from under mom and dad's fold completely first. But I see that having this child will make me just have to move a little faster with everything."

"Okay man, you don't have to explain all that to me. I truly understand. I haven't told my lady much about me either. She doesn't even know I have a brother!" Dwayne laughed. "I just never know how long things are going to last in a relationship so I try not to divulge too much information too soon."

"I guess we really are brothers, huh!" They both laughed. "Well, I got to go. She doesn't know I'm coming and I don't want to get there too late. She lives with her brother and his wife and God knows what she told them about me after our conversation this morning." Dwight shook his head as they headed down the staircase to the exit.

Dwight got into his sleek black Mercedes and headed to the interstate to meet Joy. The traffic was heavy and he wished he had left much sooner. It took over four hours to make a three-hour drive, but he was happy he made it. There were always limited parking spaces available in Joy's community late at night so Dwight had to park his black Benz a few blocks from the condominiums. Dwight had stopped at a twenty-four hour grocery store to pick up some flowers for Joy. He reached into the backseat and retrieved the flowers and a card. As he walked down the street, he rehearsed what he was going to say to Joy when he saw her beautiful face. Suddenly, he caught a glimpse of a shadowy figure a few feet behind him. The person startled him slightly and he jumped from the discovery as he thought, *Where did they come from?* He turned around to try to take a better look at the person but couldn't see past the bright lamp post that was shining directly into his eyes. Dwight laughed as he regained his composure and continued down the sidewalk. He turned the corner, still a few blocks away from the condo, and heard three gunshots. He fell forward and landed face-down on the concrete. He gasped for air and felt a terrible burning sensation that went into his back and through the mid-section of his chest. He could see the beautiful yellow and red mixed roses strewn across the pavement, spattered with blood. He knew now that he had been shot and that the blood he saw was his. As he looked at the flowers, a tear fell from his eye and he thought, *Not like this, not now--what about Joy and my baby?* He couldn't move. He felt the blood seeping from his body to the ground and he could see a glimmer of red from the reflection it gave off the light shining from the lamppost. His body became cold and he began to shake. Suddenly, he tasted metal on his tongue and saw darkness approaching until there wasn't any light left to see.

Joy sat at the dining room table as Susan walked in the front door.

"How are you feeling?" Susan asked Joy.

"I'm okay. It has been a stressful day. Timothy just left with Sophie. We actually talked for a long time today, like old friends. Can you believe that?!"

"Timothy?! Wow," said Susan. "Well, I never doubted that he loved you and Sophie, Joy. He just had a problem and it was better that you left him before someone truly got hurt."

"Yeah, I know he loves me and of course it was awkward for me when he met Dwight for the first time when he visited Sophie last month. I just couldn't take being married to him anymore." Joy said with her head slumped toward the table. Susan walked past her and sat in the chair right beside her.

"Did you tell Timothy about the baby?"

"Yeah, I probably shouldn't have. It's none of his business. He has moved on with his life and I have moved on with mine. But I'm happy that he agreed to take Sophie for a while so I can sort out this whole mess. That's enough about me, Susan. How about you? How are you doing?" Joy asked.

"I'm tired. It was a long day at work and I've been ready to get home but something is going on a few blocks from here. A bunch of police and ambulances are blocking the entire street. So I was stuck in that for a while. But you know it's always something going on up the street from here. So have you talked to Dwight again?

"The phone rang all day but I'm not sure if it was him and if it were, I wouldn't have taken any of his calls anyway. He doesn't want this baby, Susan. He made that clear when I talked to him earlier. We dated for almost a year and now that I'm pregnant, it's over." Joy shook her head. "How could I have been so irresponsible?"

"Don't be so hard on yourself. How could you have known things would turn out like this? It's early, sweetie. Give him a chance to let all this digest like you have. I'm sure he'll come around. Then take it one day at a time and see what happens."

"I was taking it one day at a time. I really thought we had a good relationship. I thought he wanted to marry me some day. But instead he treated me like I meant nothing to him." Joy's eyes were red and full of tears. Susan tried her best to comfort her but knew there was nothing she could do but stand beside her and help her through this painful ordeal.

"How about Patrick and I try to talk to him?" Susan suggested.

"NO! Do not contact him! He knows how to reach me. I'll speak to him when I'm ready."

"Okay, I was just trying to help. I'll let you handle this your way."

Joy stood up from the table and stated, "Yes, let me do that" before she walked to her bedroom and closed the door.

Chapter 18 - Fight young man, fight!

AMBULANCE 16 ARRIVED at Medview Ridge Medical center in record time. The back doors slammed open as the paramedics rushed Dwight from the back of the ambulance and into the hospital emergency room, where the doctor and nurses were already waiting to help save his life. They quickly lifted Dwight's lifeless body and transferred it to the trauma operating table. Blood was everywhere as the hospital staff scrambled around the table to assist the surgeon. Dr. Wellington shouted, "We have to stop the bleeding! He has lost a lot of blood already. Blood type?"

"O negative," a nurse answered quickly.

"We need a blood transfusion and X-rays STAT! Grab the C-Arm!

"Got it! Radiology is here already, Doctor."

"We'll get it done! How many bullets are there and where are they?"

"I only see two, Doctor."

"I see them too," the doctor said. "Oh my GOD! This isn't good."

Beeeeeeeepppppppppp! The screeching sound came from the monitor.

"We have a flat line! Come on! We're not done yet! Bring him back! Come on, come on! CLEAR!" the doctor yelled as he shocked Dwight with the defibrillator. "CLEAR!" he yelled again, then shocked Dwight once more.

"Come on young man, fight! Fight for your life! Fight!" the doctor yelled as he and the nurses frantically kept working to save Dwight's life.

Chapter 19 - I'm So Sorry

JOHN DROVE AROUND the city for about thirty minutes, until he ended up at the Holiday Inn. He knew Melinda wouldn't check there for him because it wasn't high scale enough for her. During the hotel check-in, he couldn't find his wallet. He thought back and realized he left his wallet in the blazer he swung over the chair in their bedroom. He doubled back to the house and went upstairs. Melinda's silver Ferrari wasn't in the garage when he returned. He knew she shouldn't have been driving because she was wasted before he left, which was now over an hour ago now. However, he didn't concern himself with that; he just wanted to use the bathroom, grab his wallet and leave for the night. He walked out of the bathroom and there stood Melinda at the top of the staircase, looking like she had seen a ghost. Melinda gasped and stepped backwards, away from the figure that looked like John, and fell down three flights of stairs onto the marble flooring in their foyer. John lunged toward Melinda in an attempt to catch her but didn't get to her in time. He ran down the staircase, practically jumping flights. When he got to Melinda she was still conscious and talking. She kept repeating something over and over again. John leaned his ear closer to her mouth and could finally make out what Melinda was saying.

She stated, "Your sorry ass got shot, didn't you?" She repeated that over and over again.

John looked at her purse and saw her things sprawled all over the floor, including her personal nine millimeter from their personal gun locker. John turned to Melinda and screamed, "What did you do! Tell me you didn't..."

Melinda interrupted his question. She slurred as she stated, "Whatttt? Are you worried that your precious little Joy got shot too? Well, no mothafucka! YOUR sorry ass right outside that bitch's house!"

John was devastated. He knew she was still extremely intoxicated and must have thought he was a ghost. John didn't love his wife but he didn't want to see her go to jail either, so he called her father, who rushed over to their home. Matthew arrived in less than fifteen minutes and after he found out from Melinda where the shooting took place, he departed. Melinda was unconscious when the EMTs transported her to a private hospital with a concussion and multiple fractures to her ribs. She was placed in a private ward of the medical center and no one was permitted to see her according to her father, not even John. John left the hospital after Melinda was taken into surgery. He didn't want to face Matthew just yet and needed to check on Joy.

When he arrived in Joy's neighborhood, there were police cars everywhere. He parked his car a few blocks away and walked as close to the crime scene as possible. There were crime scene technicians marking some evidence they found on the ground. The victim was gone but there was a pool of blood on the ground where John suspected the victim must have laid. John also saw yellow and red roses strewn across the ground. John looked in the distance and spotted more police activity near a black Mercedes.

Could that be Dwight's car? John thought as he inched his way closer to where the vehicle was parked. From a distance he recognized the license plate. That is Dwight's car! Did she mistake Dwight for me? Did Joy get shot too? John thought then turned to discreetly flee back to his car when a detective stopped him.

"Hello, sir. I noticed you checking out the crime scene. I'm Detective Mark Otis." John tried to keep his composure although he was terrified. The only thing he could think about was getting in touch with Joy to make sure she was safe. "Yes, sir. I was stuck in the traffic jam and just wanted to see what was going on. Looks pretty bad, huh? What happened?"

Detective Otis looked at John up and down, assessing whether he looked trustworthy. He wondered if he could be a possible suspect in the crime that just occurred and concluded that he was just another privileged, nosey citizen. "Yes, it was pretty bad. A man was shot and we are in the process of interviewing witnesses now. Did you happen to see or hear anything?"

John instantly felt relief knowing it wasn't Joy that was involved. "I'm sorry, sir, but no, I just parked to see if I should go the other direction and I see now that I should."

Detective Otis reached into his pocket and retrieved a business card. "I know you said you don't have any information, Mr. Ummm..." Detective Otis hesitated, waiting for an answer from John.

"It's Bateman, Bernard Bateman," John answered as he accepted the card.

"Ok, Mr. Bateman, just for procedure, can I see some identification, please?"

John began to sweat and wondered what the hell he was thinking walking over to this crime scene. "Well, I left my wallet in my briefcase in my car. I wasn't expecting to need it. I assure you I have no idea what is going on and will gladly be on my way now."

Detective Otis glared at John and again came to the conclusion that he was just another nosey citizen. "Okay, Mr. Bateman, you can carry on but you should not make it a habit to wander into crime scenes without identification. Have a nice evening."

"Thank you, Detective." John quickly departed but walked in the opposite direction of his car. He didn't want the Detective to spot his vehicle and realize that it was similar to the victim's. John circled the block and arrived back at his car. As soon as he got in, he called Joy.

Joy answered after several rings. "Hello John, it's late; is everything okay?"

"Yes," John lied. I'm just checking on you. I was wondering how things went when you told Dwight about the baby. Did you get a chance to tell him yet?"

The phone was silent and John feared that Joy knew about the shooting that had occurred just a few blocks from her house. "Joy? Is everything okay?"

"No, it's not. He doesn't want the baby. I haven't heard anything from him since we argued this morning." John knew at that moment she had no idea what actually happened to Dwight and he decided he wasn't going to be the one to tell her. In some sick way, he felt relieved but felt sad for her at the same time. "I'm sorry to hear that." John couldn't think of anything else to say.

"John, it's late and it has been a long day. Can you call me tomorrow?"

"Sure. I'll call you tomorrow," John said as they disconnected the call. He was happy that she ended the conversation for him.

Now what to do about Melinda? he thought. John drove around aimlessly for a few hours until he received a call from Medview Ridge Medical Center requesting him to come there right away. John was only three miles from the hospital, circling it like a shark. He contemplated how he was going to see Melinda since Matthew had banned him from seeing her until he was sure the accident wasn't domestic related. So he was surprised to receive a call to come back to the hospital and wondered if it had something to do with the shooting. John had already hidden the weapon and wiped Melinda's hands as much as he could to try to eliminate the gunpowder residue he suspected was on her hands. He knew he didn't have enough time to change her clothes, but luckily, she passed out before EMS arrived to transport her. John didn't want them to witness her repeating over and over again that she had shot him. They might end up putting the shooting together with Dwight's. If she was implicated in that shooting it would lead them to John and his connection to Joy and Dwight. John refused to let that happen.

John arrived back to the hospital and was quickly ushered to Melinda's bedside. He had never seen her look so helpless. She was hooked to all types of machines. John could hear the nurse call the doctor, indicating that Mrs. Mack's husband had arrived. John had never heard Melinda's last name used without the Conglin hyphenation and it even sounded strange to his ears. As John observed tubing over Melinda's face and a tube protruding from her chest area to a small bag, he suddenly felt sorry for her. She doesn't deserve this, he thought. Why wouldn't she just let me go and take what I deserve?

A tall, slender, young doctor walked toward John and extended his hand. "Hello I'm Dr. Williams. Are you Mr. Mack?"

"Yes, I'm Mr. Mack."

Dr. Williams looked relieved and stated, "I'm glad you could make it so soon. I guess you haven't heard about Mr. Conglin?"

John looked inquisitively at the doctor but didn't say a word. So the doctor stated, "I didn't think so. Well, we will get into that later. The reason I needed to see you right away is because your wife needs emergency surgery that was initially refused."

"Ok. Surgery for what and who refused it?" John asked.

"Mr. Mack, time is of the essence here. We have placed your wife in an induced coma. She is suffering from hemorrhaging on the brain. She also has a pierced lung. Her father had initially denied the surgery based on the possibility of her not surviving it. I couldn't lie to him and tell him that there wasn't a chance of her not surviving. That wouldn't be realistic. Well, that doesn't matter now anyway, because unfortunately he can no longer make those decisions. Frankly, I don't understand why you weren't making the decision in the first place, considering you are her husband. However, we need to do something right away about the bleeding and swelling to her brain. So we need you to decide right away what you want us to do."

"Wait a minute! What do you mean he can no longer make those decisions? I don't understand."

"Mr. Mack, I am violating protocol here but for the sake of time and your wife's health, I'm going to go ahead and inform you that your father-in-law had a massive heart attack on top of the complications from pancreatic cancer. He was terminally ill and had already received a life expectancy date from another physician. So, now you are her primary guardian and we need immediate authorization to operate."

John stood quietly, staring at the tall, slender, determined man. He couldn't believe what he had just informed him about Matthew and thought he was dreaming. In that instant, he knew everything was now his. There were no successors to Matthew's fortune besides Melinda--no one else to claim the ADC throne but him.

"SIR!" the doctor stated very forcefully, knocking John out of his thoughts. "Time is of the essence. Would you like us to operate or not?"

John looked straight toward the young doctor and coldly stated, "No."

"What?" the doctor said.

"I said no. I would not like to authorize surgery at this time."

The doctor looked astonished at John's answer and said, "But that means she may die or have permanent brain damage if we don't do something right away."

"Well, Doctor, that means there is also a chance that she will be okay, right?"

"Well, yes," the young doctor stated.

"So again, I don't want her to undergo surgery. However, there is something I would like to talk to YOU about in private. Is there somewhere we can talk?"

"Yes, we can go to my office. It's right down this hallway. Follow me."

John and Dr. Williams proceeded to the doctor's office as Melinda lay helpless in the hospital bed.

After an all-night stint, John arrived back home mentally drained. His phone had been ringing all night and now he suspected it was people concerned about Matthew's death. John refused to answer the calls. He wasn't ready to deal with anything else right now. Ironically enough, Matthew was in the morgue at the same hospital where his daughter was fighting for her life. And what about Dwight? he thought. Where the hell is he?

John was thankful that it was the weekend and he had another day before making any official preparations about the death, job, Melinda or otherwise. As he climbed the stairs, he looked at a long scrape that descended from the top of the staircase banisters all the way to the bottom. He suspected Melinda must have caused it during her fall down the stairs. That crazy bitch actually tried to kill me, John thought. John immediately thought about Dwight. I need to find out if he's okay, but how? How can I check on him and keep my nose clean at the same time? What if he is dead? What if Joy finds out all of this is my fault? John began to think of all the ramifications behind his involvement. He dropped to his knees and began to scream in frustration, "Oh my God. What have I done?" His screams echoed through the empty house. "JOYYYYY, I'm so sorry!"

Chapter 20 - Mistaken Identity

DETECTIVE OTIS STOOD in the hallway outside of Dwight's hospital room like he had done so many times in the past six months. He recalled the night of the shooting, when he stood outside the operating room, anxiously awaiting the determination of Dwight's condition. Dwight had been in surgery that day for over three hours. He had lost a lot of blood after one bullet pierced his spleen and exited through his left flank. They got the bleeding under control after removing his spleen but the doctors were greatly concerned about another bullet that had lodged close to his spinal cord. The hospital staff feared the worse and were diligently trying to locate his next of kin.

Detective Otis had stopped a nurse that was exiting the operating room and asked, "Excuse me. Has the patient awakened at all since he arrived? I was just wondering if he happened to say anything about what occurred?"

"No. I'm sorry, Detective, he has been unconscious the whole time." The nurse quickly proceeded down the long corridor to another operating room.

Detective Otis' thoughts were interrupted as he saw a man he recognized from the crime scene the night of the shooting. He scratched his head and then looked over his notes to find the man's name that he jotted down in his little notebook. He remembered the clean-cut businessman snooping around the crime scene that night. Detective Otis watched as the man walked with another doctor down the hall in the opposite direction. "Mr. Bateman?" Detective Otis called out to him but he didn't answer. He called him again but this time referred to him as Bernard, but again he did not respond. Detective Otis knew the man was close enough to have heard him but the man continued down the hall and out of the facility. Detective Otis walked down the hall to see who Mr. Bateman was visiting but the area was a privately secured ward of the hospital. Detective Otis knew it could have been just a coincidence since it was six months ago, but still made a mental note to check into this Bernard Bateman after all.

Chapter 21 - Where are you Dwight

A WEEK HAD PASSED and Joy's morning sickness was at its peak. She thought about the fact that she hadn't heard from Dwight at all since their last heated conversation over the phone. She really wanted to reach out to him but each time she contemplated it she would change her mind. She finally gathered the nerve to call his local real estate investing office in Juniper but the phone only rang with no answering machine or voice mail attached. She was sure he could see her number in the caller ID and would eventually return her call. But he never called. She then attempted to contact the office in Newcomb but the number he had given her had been disconnected. A month had passed now and there was still no word from Dwight.

"Hey Patrick, I need a favor," Joy stated.

"Sure, whatever you need."

"Will you ride with me to Newcomb one day this week?"

"All the way to Newcomb, really? Why?"

"That's where I met Dwight and I would like to go to this lounge called Cantucci's to see if anyone has heard from him."

"Sure, sure just let me know when."

"Are you busy right now?" Joy looked at her big brother with puppy dog eyes.

"Joyyyyyy."

"Please, Patrick. He was usually there on this night so I'm sure if he is around I'll be able to run into him."

"Okay, let me call Susan so she won't be worried about us. That's a total of a six-hour drive back and forth, you know."

"Yes. But I need closure. And if he won't return my calls or answer the phone, I'll have to go to him."

Three hours later Patrick and Joy pulled into the parking lot at Cantucci's. She quickly scanned the parking lot for Dwight's car but did not see it anywhere. It had been over a year since she had been there. The lounge looked exactly the same, with all the chrome and silver trimming outlining the multitude of mirrors along the small dance floor. Joy and Patrick approached the bar.

"Hi, I'm Joy, and this is my brother Patrick. I really hope you remember me. Your name is Carlos, right?"

"Yes, I sort of remember your face. It has been awhile. What can I get for you two this evening?" Carlos asked.

"I was hoping you could give me some information about Mr. Moss. Does he still come to this location?"

"Why, y'all looking for him?"

"Do you know how I can reach him? Has he been in here recently?" Joy asked excitedly.

"I'm sorry, but we don't give out information on our patrons."

"So he was here," Patrick stated. "When was the last time you saw him?"

"Look, I don't want any trouble and I'm not trying to lose my job. These people pay a lot of money to come here."

"Sir," Joy pleaded, "I really need to get in touch with him and if there is any way you can help me I would appreciate it."

The man looked to his left and right then leaned in closer to Joy at the bar. "I saw him in here about a month ago. Heard he had some major family issues and haven't seen him since. He even closed his open bar account with us. So I suspect he's not coming back."

"Do you have any forwarding information?" Patrick asked.

"This place doesn't keep that type of stuff and I've said too much as it is. I'm sorry I couldn't be more help to you." The man walked to the other side of the bar to refill another patron's drink.

"This is a waste of time. He isn't here," Joy stated.

"Let's go past this real estate office and see what we find there," Patrick suggested. Joy eyes lit up with hope and they drove to the Newcomb address she had from one of his advertisement postcards.

The street was dark but Patrick and Joy could obviously see that the address listed on his postcard as his business address was just a Post Office box.

"I can't believe this, Patrick! Was anything about him real? He hasn't called in a month! Then he packed up and moved out of his Juniper office, closed his account at Cantucci's and now I find out this 'main' business of his is a damn Post Office box address! What the hell!"

"Don't go getting yourself all worked up, Joy. That's not going to help anything."

"Worked up! Worked up! Patrick, I'm pregnant! Divorced, living with you, in college with a mediocre job and now pregnant with no baby father to help me raise my child!"

"Okay, just calm down. I have an idea. Let's go try to file a missing person report. The police station is right over there." Patrick pointed across the street to a brick building with dark blue trim. He drove into the parking lot and parked.

Joy jumped out of the car first and headed into the police station. A middle-aged female desk sergeant looked up from her reading glasses as Joy approached the counter.

"Hello. I'd like to file a missing person report."

The sergeant walked to the counter, "I can try to help you with that." She walked back to her desk to retrieve a form then walked back to the counter again. "Ok, first things first, who is missing?"

"My boyfriend--well, my ex-boyfriend."

"Your ex-boyfriend?" the sergeant repeated.

"Well, he's actually my expectant child's father."

"And why do you want to file a missing person report on him, may I ask?"

"Because I haven't been able to reach him since I told him about the baby and that isn't like him, even though we had a huge argument."

"So you told him you were pregnant and you haven't seen or heard from him since? Is that correct?"

"EXACTLY!" Joy said.

"Are you two married either by the state or common law?"

"No. I said he was my boyfriend, future baby father. Whatever. Why?"

"I have to ask you, ma'am. Were you two living together?"

"No, we didn't live together. Oh my God! Are you going to help me or not?"

"Calm down, ma'am. There are a few things I have to find out first from you before filing a report and I can tell you now that I can't file this report for you."

"What? Why?" Joy looked perplexed. Patrick walked into the police station and joined Joy at the counter. "Any information yet Joy?" he asked.

"No! Not at all. She said she can't file the report for me."

The sergeant shook her head as she balled up the paper she had started writing on then tossed it aggressively in the trash. "Ma'am, if you're not married to him, a guardian for him, living with him, a blood relative such as a sister, mother or child to the person, we can't file a report. Your best bet would be to go past his house or talk to his mother or another relative to try to reach him. But this sounds like a classic case of a future dad with cold feet to me. So take a number and get in line at the child support office because I assure you they will find him before you will if he is ever found at all. Now have a nice evening." The sergeant walked back to her desk and sat down.

Patrick looked harshly at the unsympathetic sergeant, even though he knew she was right. He knew Joy wanted to jump across that counter and open a can of whoop-ass on the woman, whether she was the police or not. So he quickly grabbed her arm gently, walked out the door and headed back to the car.

The ride back to Juniper was extra quiet as Joy recapped her situation over and over again. *How did this happen to me?* she thought. *I was so happy just a few weeks ago, and now this.*

"You ok, Joy?" Patrick asked to break the awkward silence.

"I have no choice but to be all right. He just doesn't want this baby.What else could it be? I'm only a pharmacy technician part time trying to pay for college. How am I going to finish my medical degree now? Why didn't I insist on meeting his family and friends? I feel so stupid! I was an idiot to have slept with a man I didn't know a thing about, Patrick. That was so irresponsible of me. But he was so charming and good to me. I would have never thought this would happen."

Joy sat silently as Patrick drove back to Juniper. She thought about Dwight and wondered where their relationship went wrong. *We had such a promising relationship. We did everything together. I even introduced him to my daughter. What will she think? Did my relationship with John push him this far? I know he didn't approve of my close relationship with John and I pray he doesn't think this is John's baby I'm carrying. My relationship with John is strictly platonic. Maybe I should have pushed John away and discontinued communicating with him. NO! Am I crazy? There is absolutely NO REASON for Dwight to walk out on me now. It doesn't matter if John were hanging around. After all this deception on his part, it's time for me to toughen up and move on. He made his decision and I have to live with it. I'm glad I still have John as a good friend. John has been here for me since the first day he had his prescription filled at the pharmacy. We have so much more than Dwight and I ever had, even without the sex! I knew we had something special a long time ago and now I truly see it. Friendship trumps everything. Forget you, Dwight. I will raise this baby on my own and we will be okay.*

Chapter 22 - I'm Awake Now

"DOCTOR VALLARIO, come quickly!" the young nurse yelled down the long corridor. "Mrs. Mack has awakened from her coma!"

The doctor rushed down the hallway into a huge private room situated at the end of the hall. He grabbed the medical jacket and quickly read the patient's name. The nurse was correct. The patient had awakened. Doctor Vallario walked closer to the patient and couldn't believe his eyes. *It's Melinda,* he thought.

"Melinda. Can you hear me?" he asked. Melinda moved her head slowly from side to side then opened her eyes to a squint.

Doctor Vallario turned to the young nurse and said, "Go page Dr. Williams immediately."

"Yes sir," she stated as she rushed out the room.

Doctor Vallario turned back toward Melinda then turned to the multitude of monitors positioned to check her vitals. He didn't work at the hospital on a regular basis. He was semi-retired but would come to the hospital to help out from time to time. If he had known Melinda was there, he would have been there every day. He had a strong attachment to this patient. This wasn't just any patient by far. He watched as she laid there, looking helpless and trying to speak. He was in awe of her resemblance to her mother, who was his first true love. He attempted to erase her mother from his thoughts as he began to check Melinda's vital signs. Melinda tried to speak. Her throat was dry and extremely scratchy. Finally, she formed three words. "Where am I?"

Her voice was strained and raspy. She slowly began to rub her throat.

"I'm Doctor Vallario and you're in Medview Ridge Medical Center."

Melinda looked surprised then asked, "Hos-hospital. Why?"

"I have to review your medical jacket further but it appears you suffered from a fall of some type."

"How long have I been here?" she asked, concerned. Doctor Vallario looked at the admittance date on her records and stated, "It appears it's been over six months."

Melinda turned and looked directly at the doctor. "Did you say over six months?"

Before Doctor Vallario could answer, Doctor Williams walked into the room.

"Well hello, Mrs. Mack. I'm doctor Theodore Williams. I was assigned to oversee your condition. It is wonderful to see you have awakened finally. Let me speak with some of my staff in the hall for just a minute and I will be back to answer any questions you may have." Doctor Williams motioned for most of the staff except for Doctor Vallario to step into the hallway.

Melinda attempted to sit up in the bed. *What happened to me?* She tried to think back to what caused her injuries but couldn't recall a thing. She rubbed her head and looked around the room. She could see Doctor Vallario intently reviewing her medical jacket at the foot of her bed. There were a number of old Mylar balloons that read *Get Well Soon* half-floating in the corner. There were a number of greeting cards push-pinned to the wall as well. Melinda looked down at her nails that were all natural and extra-long. She managed to sit up and painfully move her legs to the edge of the bed. She could now feel that she had a catheter between her legs. Her body felt heavy and numb. Her muscle movement was sporadic but she was determined to try to stand.

Doctor Vallario glanced up from the medical jacket to find Melinda attempting to step off the bed. "Noooo!" he screamed. "You can't possibly walk yet. You will hurt yourself." Doctor Williams and the rest of the staff heard the commotion and ran back into the room.

Melinda started to panic and yelled as loud as she could at the doctor, "I've got to get out of this bed. I have to see myself! Take this catheter out of me! Disconnect this stuff! I'm okay; let me go! Where's my father? He will take care of all of you and all of this!"

Doctor Vallario looked at Doctor Williams for the answer to her question before Doctor Williams stated, "Melinda, that's another story. I regret to inform you that your father passed while you were in your coma." Melinda started breathing heavily, her blood pressure began to rise on the monitor and she started convulsing.

"She's having a seizure!" Doctor Vallario yelled before he sprang into action to save Melinda. He noticed that the nurses jumped right in after him but Doctor Williams did not. After Melinda stopped convulsing, Doctor Vallario shot Doctor Williams a dirty look.

Doctor Williams ignored Doctor Vallario's obvious negative view of deciding to tell Melinda about her father and not helping during the medical emergency. Instead of commenting, Doctor Williams motioned a nurse to his side and told her to sedate Melinda for the rest of the night. He took Melinda's medical jacket out of Doctor Vallario's hands and said, "Thank you, but I'll tend to my patient now if you don't mind."

Doctor Vallario gave Doctor Williams another dirty look and stated, "That's what you should have done less than a minute ago when she was convulsing. Thank God I was here." The nurses looked at one another in response to the exchange but didn't say a word as Doctor Vallario walked out of the hospital room.

Doctor Williams stayed with Melinda until she fell asleep. He had excused all the other staff and wanted to ensure himself that her vitals and all necessary paperwork were perfect before he ended his rounds for the evening. He went to his office and sat at his desk then looked up at the ceiling in thought, *What went wrong? How did she awaken today? How in the hell am I going to tell him she's awake!* Doctor Williams picked up his phone and slowly dialed John's number.

"Hello, John? It's Theodore. Look we really need to talk about Melinda's condition. I can't continue to keep her like this. You really need to make a decision before something happens and she wakes up unexpectedly!"

"Are you telling me you're not capable of keeping her induced anymore, Theodore? I haven't finished my transition yet, so you have to hold off a little longer."

"John, it's been six months now. I'm surprised I've been able to get away with it this long."

"Theodore, just keep the bitch under, okay? I need you to make sure she stays that way for a few more months, at least. Then I'll decide if I want her to wake up at all." Suddenly, Doctor Williams heard a noise outside his office.

"I have to go," said Dr. Williams. "I'll talk to you later." He hung up the phone lightly and crept to the door of his office to peek into the hallway. He looked up and down then exited his office and checked the adjoining offices but didn't find anyone in sight. *I must have been hearing things,* he thought as he went back into his office.

Doctor Vallario stood in the back staircase adjacent to Doctor Williams' office. He held his breath and then held the door to prevent it from squeaking again after he listened to Doctor Williams' call to John. He wasn't expecting Doctor Williams to still be there and wanted to check Melinda's medical file a little more thoroughly. When Doctor Williams went back to his office, Doctor Vallario quietly closed the stairwell door all the way then went back down to Melinda's room to check on her. Melinda was still heavily sedated so he assigned someone on his own staff to aggressively monitor her. *What happened to you, child, and where is your mother?* Dr. Vallario pondered his next thought then said to himself, "I think it's time find your mother."

Doctor Vallario never showed up to work before ten, but today he was determined to find out what was going on with Melinda's case and needed to catch her awake before Doctor Williams sedated her again. He went straight to her room and found that she was awake but still a little groggy. "Melinda?" he said. "Melinda. Can you hear me? It's very important that you try to understand me."

Melinda slowly opened her eyes and looked at the doctor. She could see the concern in his eyes and immediately felt a boost of energy. She groggily answered, "Yes, Doctor."

"You don't have to talk, just listen! This is a matter of life and death! Your life and your death! Do you understand me?"

Melinda perked up even more. "Okay," she said.

"I need you to act as though as you don't remember anything but people! Okay? I don't have much time to talk but it's imperative that you act as though as you don't remember anything that happened the night you were injured."

"Okay, I can do that. Why am I doing it and why are you doing this for me?"

"Honestly, dear, I don't know why you don't need to remember but I believe it will save your life. As far as why I'm doing it for you, I'm not. I'm doing it for your mother. Now you follow instructions and everything should be okay. I have to leave. I don't want them to keep seeing me around you, but keep your eyes open and stay sharp."

"Okay." Melinda said weakly as she watched the short, grey-haired old doctor leave the room.

Melinda sat up in the bed and thought of the night she was injured. At this point she remembered everything. She recalled following John to his car and watching him speed off into the night. She recalled going to their gun safe and removing her pistol and placing it in her purse. She recalled getting in her car and heading toward Joy's house and spotting the black Mercedes parked a few blocks away from Joy's house. She remembered getting out of the car and spotting a man that looked like John walking in the opposite direction holding flowers. She recalled pulling her gun out of her purse and pointing it in his direction and last, she remembered hearing three gunshots before running back to her car and heading back to her house only to find John standing in their bedroom. *How the hell?* she thought. Then she smiled and shook her head.

Then she thought about Joy and the baby. *I've been here for six months! That means she's six or seven months pregnant with my husband's baby! OH HELL NO! I'll take care of that!*

Dr. Williams walked into the room and interrupted Melinda's angry thoughts. "Good morning, Mrs. Mack."

"Conglin-Mack," Melinda corrected him.

"Yes, I apologize, Conglin-Mack," Dr. Williams repeated. "I see you're definitely getting better."

Melinda sensed the sarcasm in his statement. "We need to have a serious conversation, Dr. Williams."

"Ok, sure. I'm right here. What's on your mind?"

"You will no longer be my lead physician; Dr. Vallario will. Also, I would like to know what type of relationship you have with my husband."

"Dr. Williams began to stutter as he answered Melinda, "What, what do you mean?"

"Did he hire you to care for me personally?" Melinda asked.

"Well, yes he wanted to provide you with the best..."

Melinda cut off his statement as she said, "You will no longer be my lead physician. You can leave now." Melinda shooed him away and lay back down and turned toward her television. She could hear the doctor quickly leave and then a few seconds later she heard someone enter her room. She turned around, ready to jump into Dr. Williams' behind, only to see a different man standing at the doorway wearing a cheap brown suit and hat.

"Hello, are you Mrs. Bateman?" the man asked.

"No, not at all. Why do you ask?"

"Well, I saw Mr. Bateman leave from this area and was trying to figure out which hospital suite he came from."

"Well sir, why don't you just ask him? I don't know a Mr. Bateman and this is a private ward so I'm sure you're not supposed to be here anyway," Melinda said as she pushed the red button to summon the nurse.

"I'm just trying to get some information from him, that's all."

"I already told you I don't know him. I would appreciate it if you would leave now."

"Not a problem, ma'am. Sorry to disturb you." Detective Otis tilted his hat towards Melinda as he backed out of the room but not before taking note of her name from the medical jacket that was in a slot at the end of her bed. A nurse entered the room as Detective Otis walked out and down the hall. "Is everything okay, Mrs. Mack?"

"Conglin-Mack!" Melinda snapped. "No. Everything is not okay. This is supposed to be a private ward but a strange man just visited me today. Can you make sure that never happens again, please?"

"Yes ma'am, but he must have already been in this ward because no one can get in without clearance first. All the doors are secured. I'll go check for you."

"That will not be necessary. Just advise the desk to not let anyone just wander into my ward, please. I would greatly appreciate that."

"Not a problem. The nurse left the room as Melinda recounted the brief conversation with the man who never gave his name. *He called me Mrs. Bateman. Why does that name ring a bell? I can't place it right now, but I know it means something. Oh well, I figured the cops would come asking questions. I'm not saying a thing to them or to John. I'm going to let them keep believing what they want to believe until I can use it to my advantage! As far as I'm concerned I don't remember nothing!*

Chapter 23 – The Investigation

DETECTIVE OTIS WALKED back out the private ward and down the corridor to another room he frequently visited. He longed for the day he could talk to his prime witness, the man who had been fighting for his life for six months now. The man who slept silently in a vegetative state. The man identified as Mr. Dwight Moss. His brother and parents visited him at least once a week. Unfortunately, no one could explain why someone would want to hurt Dwight. Dwayne approached the detective and asked him the same question he asked every time he saw him. "Have you been able to locate Joyce?"

Detective Otis had been diligently trying to locate a woman named Joyce, which Dwayne thought was Joy's name. Dwayne had completely heard his brother incorrectly and unfortunately Detective Otis couldn't locate Joy without a last name and with an incorrect first name.

"No, Mr. Moss. I'm sorry but I couldn't get a match on any pregnant Joyces in that area. Dwayne was disappointed and felt the woman in his brother's life had something to do with him being shot that night. Dwayne looked at the detective and said, "Thank you but please keep looking. My brother said he had a fight with this woman and there is a child on the way. I want to make sure she knows he wanted to make things right between them and make sure that the baby is well taken care of. At this point, I don't even know if she did it! But detective, that's the only lead I have."

Detective Otis looked at Dwayne, who was a spitting image of the man lying on the bed fighting for his life and knew he had to figure out what happened to him that night. "I'll do everything I can, Mr. Moss. I can't make any promises."

"That's all I ask of you, Detective." Dwayne said as he walked back into the room holding the ring his twin brother bought to give Joy.

Dr. Williams hurried back to his office to call John. He dreaded making the call but knew he had no choice at this point. He listened as the phone rang twice before John answered. "Hello."

"Hello John, this is Theodore. I have some troubling news for you."

"Yes, Doctor Williams, I suspected that since it's so early. What's going on? Is everything still working out as planned?"

"Well, no, not really. She awakened and pretty much fired me today," the doctor reluctantly stated.

"Awakened! How did that happen! I pay you too damn much money to keep that bitch asleep and you call me first thing in the morning telling me she has risen from the dead!"

"Please calm down, John," the doctor said nervously. "Believe me, I'm just as concerned as you are. I could go to jail and lose my license for this. We have to keep a calm head right now."

"Calm my ass, Doc! I have a lot riding on this and it takes time to make the moves I'm trying to make. I need you to put that bitch back to sleep until I'm finished. Understand?"

"That might not be possible, John. I told you we should have just got rid of her in the first place and that this could happen."

"How the hell did you let her wake up, Theodore? "How much have I paid you? How much?! Did someone come behind your back and wake her up? I told you I needed at least year to complete the company takeover but NOOO!"

"Don't blame me, John. I didn't want a murder on my hands, just like you didn't want one on yours. That's why you didn't finish her off a long time ago."

"Okay, well I'm going to go talk to her today to see where her head is."

"Okay, but I think it's best if I leave altogether, John. Can you just pay me the rest of the money and I can move on from all this before everything blows up in my face? I've done my part."

John was quiet for a minute as he thought about Dr. Williams' request then answered, "You know what, that's a good idea. I'll have the money tomorrow. I'll see you around 10am."

John hung up the phone and got dressed. He had plans to see Joy for lunch but knew he had to cancel again to handle this situation. He hadn't seen Joy much recently with everything that had been going on, but he had every intention to continue seeing her. He just needed to complete his mission to get as much of ADC's interest as possible.

John headed out the door to the hospital. He arrived at the hospital not knowing what to expect. This was the first time he had seen Melinda awake since the night she fell down the stairs. As he walked in the door he was surprised to see Melinda sitting upright in the bed brushing her own hair. She turned to look at John and a huge smile spread across her face. "Hi baby!" Melinda said as she reached her arms out for a hug.

John was completely confused, but replied, "Melinda. How are you feeling?"

"Never better. I can't wait to come home! I miss you so much!"

John looked at Melinda and thought, *Damn, she really did hit her head!* But he said, "Well I'm sure the doctors have a lot to take care of before you can be released from here."

Melinda smiled angelically at John and said, "No, not really. They told me they just need to run a few more tests and continue rehabilitation for my muscle functions but other than that I'm okay. Isn't that just wonderful, John?"

John hesitated and said, "Yeah, I guess so. So tell me, Melinda, do you remember anything about what happened that night?"

"No," Melinda said then made a fake sad face. "I wish I did, but it's okay because I'm okay and I can go on and live my life."

"You mean you don't remember ANYTHING at all?" John said in surprise.

"No, I don't. I remember us staying at some beautiful resort and I remember us making love. I remember my father slightly, but not much of anything else. Maybe one day you can fill in the blanks for me. I don't even know if I really want to know," Melinda said and made a sad face. Then she looked back up at John and said, "I know I just love you so much and can't wait to get back to living. I've lost six months of my life, including the loss of my father. I don't want to lose anything else."

John looked at Melinda, still completely confused, but was convinced for the moment that she didn't remember anything that happened. Melinda motioned for John to come closer to the bed. He walked closer and Melinda pulled him close to hug him. John hugged her back as Dr. Williams walked into the room. John looked at Dr. Williams, who looked surprised as well at the sight of the couple embracing.

"John, I'm glad you could make it," Dr. Williams stated. John and Melinda released their embrace and Melinda smiled at Dr. Williams and said, "Hello, Doctor. How is your day going?"

"It's going just fine, Mrs. Conglin-Mack."

"Oh, just call me Melinda," she said with a smile. John and Dr. Williams quickly glanced at each other.

"Okay, Melinda," the doctor said reluctantly. "John and I need to discuss your case and come up with some decisions on where it would be best for you to undergo your rehabilitation."

"No, that won't be necessary, Doctor. I'll be going home with John this week and we will hire someone to handle everything from our estate. Isn't that right, John?" Melinda looked at John with a genuinely excited face.

John looked back at the doctor inquisitively and said, "I guess, if you feel it's safe for her to return to the estate, I don't have a problem with those arrangements."

Melinda continued with her big plastered smile, "Great! Then it's settled. Sign my discharge papers, Doctor. It's time for me to go!" Melinda smiled as she looked from John to the doctor and back to John. She knew neither wanted her to be discharged but she was determined to get out of her deathbed and back to her world, and no one was going to stop her.

Chapter 24 - Unexplained Misfortune

THE WINTER MONTHS were rolling in and classes at the university were going on break. Joy welcomed the much-needed break. She was almost eight months pregnant now and walking around campus was becoming more difficult by the day. Joy thought of how she would continue school and take care of a newborn baby and Sophie alone. She decided online classes were the easiest way to avoid falling too far behind in her studies. She knew she couldn't take all of her necessary classes toward her degree online, but just taking a few would bring her that much closer to reaching her goals.

Joy attempted to enroll for the upcoming semester, but her student loan was immediately denied without an explanation. She never fell behind on her student loan payments or failed a class. A few days later she received a certified letter that stated she was over $50,000 in debt with the university. Joy went to the registration office to find out what was going on. She explained that she hadn't even taken $50,000 worth of classes at the university. The young attendant handed Joy a packet of paperwork to fill out. She said they must conduct an internal investigation of her transcript history. Joy requested to see her transcript while she was in the registrar's office and found numerous erroneous classes. Joy told the registrar that she had never taken the majority of the classes that were listed on that transcript and that it must belong to someone else. The lady told Joy again that she must fill out all the information in the packet and submit it to be reviewed and that there was nothing else she could do to help her until they determined their findings.

Joy was at a loss. She felt she had no choice but to do as the lady instructed and wait for them to find out that she was not the person who made this debt. Joy walked back to her car feeling defeated and frustrated. She began to cry as she sat behind the wheel of her car. She thought, *First Dwight, then my job and now my student loan--what else can go wrong?*

She drove back to her brother's condo in tears, face flushed and breathing heavily. She parked and as she attempted to exit the car, she felt a terrible cramp in the bottom of her stomach. She had been out all day trying to take care of this nonsense, to no avail, and believed she had overexerted herself. She sat back down in the car and then she felt the cramp again. This time it frightened her with its intensity and she wondered if her baby was okay. When the pain subsided, she attempted to depart the car again when a woman walked up to her and asked if she was okay. Joy looked at the woman, who was very pretty and poised. The woman reached out her hand to help Joy exit the vehicle. Joy welcomed the help as she grimaced at the sharper pain she now felt menacing in her lower abdomen. The woman grabbed hold of Joy's arm and helped her walk to the condo.

When they entered the condo they realized no one was home. Joy wondered where her brother was because he was normally home by now. Joy sat down on the couch while holding her stomach in pain. The woman looked at Joy and stated, "Let me get you something to drink." She came back with a glass of water and insisted that Joy drink it down. But the water didn't help at all; it just seemed to make things worse. Joy started cramping more and more until finally the lady said, "I'm sorry, but I have to leave. I hope you'll be okay."

Joy watched as the lady left the condominium before she could even get her name to say thank you. Joy tried to make it to her bedroom to lie down when the cramps became worse. She began to sweat profusely and started to feel lightheaded. Joy reached for the phone as quickly as she could and called 911. She tried to call Patrick as well but her vision became too blurry to see the numbers on the phone. Soon she could hear the ambulance heading her way, but unfortunately, before they reached the condo she collapsed to the floor.

Paramedics knocked and knocked on the door but Joy was unconscious. The dispatcher attempted to call the home but the line was busy. The fire department responded and forcefully opened the door and found Joy lying only a few feet from the door on the floor with the phone receiver in her hand. They quickly started CPR and transported her to the ambulance to head to the hospital. Melinda sat in her car and watched as the paramedics put Joy in the ambulance. "Let's see who dies now, bitch!" she stated as the ambulance pulled out of sight.

Patrick was sitting in his office when he received the frightening call from the hospital. A nurse stated that his number was found among Joy's personal belongings and wanted to know if he was Joy's next of kin. He stated, "Yes. I'm her brother." He was advised to report to the hospital immediately so he dropped everything, called his wife Susan, and raced to his car.

On the drive to the hospital, he thought about all the stress Joy had been under in the past few weeks. He was happy that Timothy finally stepped up as a man and father and started to help her more with Sophie. He still attempted to keep Joy strong and tried to free her mind of worry while carrying the baby, but he knew his sister was very independent and hated to have to rely on him and his wife. He had helped her file all the mounds of necessary papers to refute the many claims of fraud that had been brought against her. He knew it bothered Joy that he and Susan supported them so much but she needed it after losing her job and after social services discontinued her benefits. But the crazy part to them was that there was no reason for any of the problems to be happening in the first place. Every allegation Joy faced was false. No one could explain what was truly going on. He did everything he could to keep Joy as comfortable and stress free as possible so he wasn't thrilled to learn she was in the hospital.

Patrick arrived in record time. As he entered Joy's hospital room, he watched his little sister sleep peacefully with an oxygen mask covering her face. The nurse walked into the room and asked if he was the father of the child and Patrick quickly explained who he was. When Joy opened her eyes, the largest smile spread across her weary face. She looked around the room.

"Hey Button. How you feeling?" Patrick asked Joy.

"I'm okay, I think," she muttered as clearly as she could through the oxygen mask while nodding her head. The nurse walked over to assist her with her mask.

"Let me take that off for a while," the nurse said.

"Thank you," replied Joy. "Excuse me, ma'am." Joy motioned the nurse as she was departing the room.

"Yes dear?" The nurse looked at her with an eagerly helpful expression.

Joy stuttered as she asked, "Is, is, is my baby okay?"

The nurse looked endearing at Joy as she walked over and held her hand before she said, "Yes. Your baby is perfectly fine. But you, on the other hand, need to slow down because you were unconscious and your blood pressure was extremely high when they brought you in here. We were finally able to wake you and then you started vomiting violently and fainted again. But the doctor will be in soon to talk to you. Okay?"

"Wow!" Joy exclaimed. "I THREW UP AND FAINTED!"

The nurse nodded her head. "Well, I have to check on some other patients. If you need anything, pull the string or push the red button on your bed and I'll come running." The nurse left the room.

Joy sat up in the bed and looked at Patrick with gazing eyes.

"Are you ok?" Patrick asked.

"Yes. That's just so weird," Joy said. "There was a lady with me, though. She walked up to my car and helped me make it to the condo, but you weren't there and I was in a lot of pain."

"I'm glad someone helped you, but I wish she hadn't left you like that. She should have called someone first," Patrick said as he looked in concern at his sister.

Joy lay back in the bed and looked at the ceiling trying to recall the events that led up to the hospital. But everything seemed to be a blur. She couldn't remember the lady's face and didn't recall getting her name either. Joy's baby's heart monitor began to alarm. Patrick looked concerned as the nurse rushed back into the room. "What's going on?" the nurse asked? "Oh my, it's the baby!" the nurse said as she rushed out of the room to get a doctor.

Joy watched the nurse sprint out the door as she screamed behind her, "Oh my God! What's wrong, I'm only seven months!" But the nurse didn't answer Joy as she disappeared from her sight down the hallway in search of a doctor.

"It's a healthy baby girl," Dr. Rhodes stated calmly as she made all safety precautions and passed the new baby to the nurses. Joy was relieved to have given birth at full term after her miscarriage scare at seven months. Joy recalled how afraid she was when her baby's heart rate dropped drastically in minutes. The doctors couldn't explain why until they took a toxicology test and found some unknown chemicals in Joy's bloodstream. They immediately put her on fluids and another medication to counter the effects of the chemicals found. Joy insisted that she hadn't taken anything and definitely didn't want to hurt herself or her baby. But the doctors weren't convinced and placed her on bed rest with extra attention for the duration of her pregnancy. They became concerned for her mental health after learning about all the stress she had been through recently. The doctors believed Joy was having major hallucinations and could end up suffering from post-partum depression as well. She was assigned a social worker for the baby to monitor her maternal progress and growth.

The nurse placed the new baby on Joy's chest and a tear dropped from Joy's eyes. She smiled as the little wrinkled body she had just given birth to squirmed softly on her chest. Joy said one word: "Sonya." All these months Joy hadn't thought of what she would name her child. She didn't even know if it were a boy or girl. She was too busy running around taking care of business before she was hospitalized and after that she just imagined what life would be like if Dwight was around. She knew her hospital bill would be ridiculous and she didn't have the money to pay for anything. But as she looked into her child's eyes, she knew everything would be okay.

The nurses removed the infant from Joy's chest, cleaned and wrapped her in a little blanket like a cocoon, then placed her in the warmer. Three days later Patrick picked up Joy and Sonya to bring them back to the condo. "Finally home," Joy said to little Sonya who appeared to understand but didn't have a clue. Sonya looked up from her carrier with the biggest, brightest eyes to be only a few days old. The social worker accompanied them to the residence to ensure the home was safe and sufficient for an infant. She asked Sophie a number of questions that Joy felt were inappropriate but she didn't say a word. The social worker found the home acceptable and said she would visit weekly for six months or until the state deemed it no longer necessary. Joy thought, *It's not necessary now* but simply said, "Okay" to the social worker as she closed the door.

Chapter 25 - A New Life

JOHN ARRIVED HOME after a long business trip. He had been working double-time since Matthew's death. He was eager to see Joy, whom he hadn't spoken to as much since Melinda got out the hospital. Melinda seemed like a different person nowadays. She was friendlier and more outgoing. Her attitude wasn't as nasty. She wasn't as controlling and she didn't seem as stuck up as before. John equated the change in behavior to have a lot to do with the absence of her father. He knew a lot had changed in Melinda's life since she awakened from the coma. She went through strenuous rehabilitation with Doctor Vallario, who personally took over her case. Melinda had successfully regained all her strength.

But unbeknownst to John, her strength and determination mainly came from wondering about John, Joy and the new baby she thought they had together. She was like a brand new woman, ready to fight. Doctor Vallario played a pivotal role in her recovery as he gave her insight as much as possible about Doctor Williams and John's attempt to keep her in a coma. Doctor Vallario could never prove it but Melinda trusted him after he told her about the longstanding friendship he had with her estranged mother, Melody. They never saw eye to eye and after she left her with her father when she was fifteen, she never spoke to her again.

She and John seemed to have developed a true relationship since he believed she didn't recall anything about the day of the accident but of course, it was all a lie. John had since become the number one man at ADC. He had full support of all the board members on the board of directors. They respected him and felt the company was in good hands with him at the helm. John's productivity had tripled since Matthew's death and that was because of the many company changes that he couldn't have made before Matthew's death. Since John's takeover you could expect a new contract to be enacted each week. John was literally "THE MAN" at the company now. Melinda, on the other hand, quickly learned how people's loyalty turns. The men who followed her father now followed John. They didn't respect anything she had to say when it came to the business because she was never involved before. Now, Melinda regretted not learning about the business. She now felt she should have stood by her father's side in the board room. She held her head high and said, "I'm a Conglin! All this is mine and I will make sure it stays that way!" She had to regain her leverage and she knew just how she was going to do it. Melinda had a mental to-do list written in blood. *I'm back, bitches! Yes! Daddy, it's audit time!*

Chapter 26 - If Only You Knew

TIME PASSED SO QUICKLY, Joy thought as she reviewed the college credit course catalog. They had finally cleared the fraud allegation and now Joy was contemplating just getting away from Juniper altogether. She had applied to a university in Newcomb and was accepted right away. She tried to convince herself that the hope of running into Dwight wasn't a driving force in her wanting to move there, but she knew she was only lying to herself.

After Dwight stopped contacting Joy, she had grown rather fond of John. She thought he was fond of her as well until he started staying away. She figured he didn't want to be burdened with a woman and her two children twenty-four-seven. So she and her cousin Charlene in Newcomb talked about her moving there.

She knew moving to another state would be difficult with two children on her own. She would need reliable child care even though Charlene insisted her mother, Ruth, wouldn't mind helping out in the beginning.

Sonya was crawling around, getting into everything, then turned and smiled in Joy's direction. "How about we go to the park while Sophie's in school, little one?" Joy said as she smiled at the little reflection of Dwight staring at her.

Joy picked up Sonya and gathered her things and headed out with Sonya. She stopped at the mailbox then saw a woman she frequently passed in the condominium development. The woman was a little older than Joy and she always smiled and seemed friendly. Joy thought she had seen her before but couldn't recall from where, then always dismissed it. Joy had never been the neighborly type, but would respond with a short hello and usually kept moving to her destination.

This time the lady stopped in front of Sonya's stroller, practically blocking her path. She started smiling and baby-talking to Sonya, who reciprocated the actions. Joy defensively looked at the woman who was now touching her child's little feet. The woman noticed Joy's reservations and stopped but introduced herself with the usual smile. "Hi, I'm MeMe," Melinda said. "Your daughter is gorgeous."

Joy reluctantly smiled back and introduced herself as well. "I'm Joy. Nice to meet you."

"What a nice name. Well, I'm just house-sitting in unit 210A for some friends and I thought I'd introduce myself," Melinda lied.

"Well, I live in unit 110B," Joy continued.

"Oh ok, you and her father live there?"

Joy knew she was trying to pry about her daughter's paternity. "No, my daughter's father doesn't live with us. It's just my daughters and me."

Joy turned to Sonya, who had started getting fidgety in her stroller. "Well, okay. It was nice to meet you. I'm sure I'll see you around," Joy said to Melinda. Although she was thinking, *I'm sure I'll see your nosey ass around.*

Melinda said, "Yes. I'm sure you will. If you ever need a babysitter I'm more than welcome to help you out; here, take my number. Just let me know ahead of time, okay?" Melinda jotted down her number on a torn-off circular paper she retrieved from the mailbox.

Joy took the number smiled and said, "Well, thank you" even though she had no intention of letting her child stay with the stranger.

"Okay, again, just let me know," Melinda stated then headed down the hallway in the opposite direction after giving Sonya one last wink and smile. Joy thanked the nice woman and walked down the hallway, pushing Sonya in the stroller through the door and toward the neighborhood park.

So that little pretty bitch thinks she is just going to have my husband's baby, kill me off, take my company and live happily ever after. She is so dumb she doesn't even know who I am, Melinda thought as she walked down the hallway to the empty condo she rented just to keep an eye on Joy and her little family. *I can't believe she still had that damn baby after all that poison I put in that damn water! Damn!*

Things are so much better between John and me now but fuck him now! If he knew what I was doing, he would have an absolute fit! But he doesn't know because he doesn't think I remember anything. Well, I do! I remember it all and there is hell to pay! As long as Wilbur continues to tell me that John is dealing with Joy, I will continue to screw up her life.

I'm the reason she can't find a job or keep one! I'm the reason her checks keep getting cut off! And I'm the reason her credit is all screwed up and she can't qualify for that measly student loan! Whatever I want is at my fingertips! They thought my father was bad! Well they haven't seen anything! That bitch is gonna realize the hard way that this town and everything in it is mine, including John. The best thing about it is she doesn't even have a clue right now. So congratulations, John, thanks to you everything in her life that she attempts to do will fail! Everyone she loves will turn on her, and I have the power to make all that happen and more! I'll take care of you as well, John. Oh, yes. Your snake ass will be duly punished for treating me like this and for killing my father! You can guarantee that! Melinda gritted her teeth as she glanced back hatefully toward the playground. Melinda spat as she closed the door to the unfurnished condo. She walked over to the balcony where she could see the neighborhood park with Joy and Sonya sitting on the bench. Amazingly enough, she hadn't caught a glimpse of her husband visiting the condo yet, but she was certain she would.

***

Wilbur sat in his office under mounds of paperwork he received from Melinda. His initial impression of her being daddy's little girl, spoiled brat, dumb broad had faded in the past months of him working to help her gain control of her father's company. He found countless large deposits to a Bernard Bateman. He ran several background checks and could not locate any information on the company this Mr. Bateman worked for. The company checks were all cashed, but they were seemingly untraceable. Wilbur knew how precise Melinda could be and didn't want to reveal what he found until he could identify where the money was going.

One thing he could attest to was that John was no longer seeing Joy as much as before. He had stopped the random stalking and photo taking and didn't interact with the baby either. Wilbur wouldn't reveal that to Melinda either, because the affair had been his meal ticket for over a year now. Wilbur wondered what happened to the other man who used to frequent Joy and noticed another man coming around more often picking up her oldest daughter. Wilbur surmised that must be the other girl's father. Wilbur was now making a nice fifteen thousand a month working for Melinda. He no longer contacted her every six hours and they had established a good working relationship. *The woman is just damaged goods,* he thought. *Rich ass damaged goods, though. I'll hang in here with her as long as I can.*

***

"Hello, Joy?"

"John? Wow! Hey, stranger. How have you been?" Joy answered excitedly.

"I'm well. Just been really, really busy at work. I'm better now though because I can imagine that beautiful smile wrapped around your face."

"Oh really? You have always been busy, John, but you were never too busy for our friendship. I mean I definitely appreciate the checks you send for me and the girls--that is so nice, but seeing you would be nice as well."

John loved the way Joy opened up to him now and longed to move forward with a relationship. However, he wanted to finish his mission at ADC and figure out what to do with the new and improved Melinda first. He still had the prenuptial agreement to deal with but felt his plan would get him enough money to ignore the forced agreement anyway.

"Nothing has changed, Joy. I'm still not too busy for you and the girls. Just need some time to sort a lot of things out at the office. I had to get rid of some dead weight and it caused me to take on more responsibilities."

"Okay, I understand that. Well, I have something I really need to tell you, John! You're going to be surprised."

"Okay, what's going on, lady?"

"I'm moving to Newcomb!"

"Newcomb! Why?" John was upset. He knew Dwight's family was in Newcomb and he didn't want Joy reconnecting with Dwight or his family. "Why would you want to move there?"

"Well, I was accepted at their university and I found a little apartment in Harmony Square too. I have everything already set up and ready to go in two weeks! I don't have much to move anyway, so a box truck will do the trick."

"Did you say in two weeks, Joy?"

"Yessss. I haven't had a chance to really sit down and talk with you like we used to. I really miss that. But I think it's time I move on from Juniper. It's for the best."

"I'll help you move. Let me know what day you want to go and I'll be there," said John.

"That's great, John! I'll let you know. Well, I have to go now. It's time to feed the children. I can't wait to see you, John," Joy said before hanging up the phone.

John was dazed all day at the thought of Joy moving on. It was time to make his move with Joy and end his marriage to Melinda. John left work early for a change to find a big black Suburban parked in front of the estate. So John drove to the opposite side of the mansion and parked. He entered the side entrance and could hear a male's voice in the distance. He also heard Melinda's voice. As he inched closer to the study, he could clearly make out their conversation. He could tell now that the man was a hired private detective who claimed John was having an affair with Joy. Melinda laughed as she told the investigator how she met with Joy in front of her condo but she didn't know who she was. The investigator laughed as well, and John was furious. He then heard Melinda call the man Wilbur. She asked him if he had learned anything new about the Bateman man. Wilbur stated no but he was working on it. John knew it was time to tie off all loose ends! *They're going to find out about the money!* he thought. *It's time to go for real.*

John left back out the side door and headed back to his office. He prepared several large checks and mailed them all to different places. Then he headed to Newcomb to find Harmony Square to cancel Joy's apartment like he had canceled the last one she leased.

Later that night John arrived home. Melinda was nowhere to be found. She hadn't called him all day and John wondered what she was up to. He now knew she was lying about not remembering anything, and it was time to activate his escape plan. John headed upstairs to pack and opened his secret safe to find it had been discovered. *That damn private detective must have found it!* he thought. *That's okay; I took all the pertinent stuff out of it anyway!*

As John exited the closet, Melinda walked up behind him and said, "Looking for something?" John turned around to see Melinda standing there looking like the old evil Melinda he was used to. "I saw you leave earlier. How much did you hear?"

"I heard enough," John answered as he grabbed a suitcase and started packing.

"Why are you running away, John? Do you think I have something on you? I thought we were doing so well nowadays," she said sarcastically. "But I see you're still fucking with that broke ass woman on the other side of town. Not to mention the fact that you're spending MY FAMILY's money on her and your bastard child!"

John swung his head around toward Melinda so quick you would have thought it was going to come off. "Child?!" he said.

"Oh, I know everything, John! Everything! You're lucky the little bastard isn't dead!"

"Melinda, that's not my child! You thought that was my child? That's ridiculous!" John scoffed.

Melinda sat the empty glass she was carrying on the mahogany desk and folded her arms. "Oh really! It's not your child, huh? Then why are you giving that bitch money! You think you're going to use me and my family, cheat on me and leave with our business! You're crazy! You're the one that's ridiculous! I'll make sure you don't see a damn dime!"

John laughed. "Melinda, we are done! And if you don't let this go and give me the divorce I want I'm going to do something you don't want me to do."

"Oh, you're threatening me now, John? You a liar, a cheat and a murderer and if you don't fix us I'll turn your ass in!" she said.

"WHAT? Murderer! How are you going to stand here and call me a murderer when it was your crazy ass that shot that man and I have the weapon to prove it?"

"So you're admitting that you know somebody was murdered, huh?"

"I'm not playing these games with your sick ass, Melinda. This is it! I swear if you bother me, Joy or her kids again, I'll turn your ass in!"

Melinda looked at John with a smirk on her face then said, "Okay, I'll give you everything you deserve. You don't have to worry about me ever again." She turned and walked out of his office and back down the hallway toward their bedroom.

John knew the other weapon was safely hidden after the night of the murder but wasn't sure if she had gotten another one while he was away. John started packing more of his things then headed to his little secret apartment until Joy was ready to make her move to Newcomb. As he arrived at the apartment he spotted a big black Suburban parked a block down the street. The Suburban resembled the one that was parked at his estate and he wondered if that was a coincidence. He entered the little half-empty apartment and went straight to the back room where he kept his photography equipment. He smiled at the mini shrine of pictures he had of Joy and all the cancelled checks piled on top of a stack of fake business contracts. *I don't need this equipment anymore. I don't see myself going back into photography like I did in my twenties with all this money I have now!*

"Good job, John. Good job!" John said, as he peeked out the window and saw the black Suburban was now gone.

***

"Hello, I would like to file a missing person report for my husband John Mack," John's wife stated as sincerely as she possibly could.

"How long has he been missing, ma'am?" the officer on the other end of the phone asked. "I haven't seen him for three days. He left for work and never came home. I'm afraid something terrible may have happened to him."

"Ok, Mrs. Mack, we will send an officer to speak with you shortly."

"Thank you." John's wife smirked as she hung up the phone. *So you finally did it, you finally left me for her.* She thought. *You just up and left me for that bitch and her bastard child! You think you got something on me but you just don't know how far I'm willing to go to get what I want. You must have forgotten who I am and about the prenuptial agreement my father made your sorry ass sign. You belong to me and you will always belong to me! My family runs this whole damn town and has connections in almost every state so you can't hide. I'll be damned if you get away with this. I helped to make you who you became. You think I made her life a living hell before? I will make it worse now. Neither one of you will find any peace as long as I'm walking this earth.* She headed into their immaculate kitchen with white quartz countertops and custom made cabinetry, then she headed to their custom made bar filled with every exotic flavor and every rare alcohol you can imagine. Her favorite was the rare white Hennessy from the islands. Mrs. Mack opened the white Hennessy and poured it into her favorite hand-blown crystal glass. As she took a sip she gazed out the expensive etched glass window to the double tiered decking that spanned over the elaborate pool that she and her husband custom designed together. *All of this! For what? All this property, money and status and I'm miserable as hell!* she thought. Melinda started to cry as the phone rang. She slowly walked over to the phone and answered. "Hello."

"Hello Melinda."

"Yes, this is she. Who is this?"

"It's your mother."

Melinda almost dropped the phone. She slowly walked back to the kitchen to make another drink then she sank into a barstool and had a long-awaited, in-depth conversation with her mother.

Chapter 27 - Present Day

JOHN HAD BEEN GONE for a week. He was happy that Joy moved away from Juniper after learning that Melinda had her tailed. He was convinced that Melinda would back off after he threatened to turn her in to the police but apparently she was still determined to not let him go. He still couldn't believe she filed a missing person report on him. He had already made up his mind to turn her in to the police if she didn't agree this time to let him go. That's the only thing he thought he could do to be rid of Melinda without killing her. John walked into the dark house. It was early and he knew Melinda was probably on the trail doing her morning run. John went into the wine cellar and opened a small compartment where he hid the gun that Melinda had in her purse the night of the shooting. He looked at the sleek nine millimeter and wondered what was going through Melinda's mind when she fired those rounds. John left the house with the gun wrapped in a towel and headed to a wooded area a few miles from where the shooting took place. He then tossed the gun in the thick brush and headed toward the airport. On his way to the airport, he called the police anonymous tip line and reported where the weapon that was used to shoot Dwight Moss was located. He also reported that Melinda was the shooter. He felt a sense of relief now that he had stashed away millions of dollars and was going to temporarily assume his old identity as Bernard Bateman and no one knew where he was going or how to find him since everyone thought Bernard died in the car accident along with John. But Bernard was never in the car the night of the accident at all. He just assumed John's identity years later as the professional architect he became. He only wished he could take Joy with him, but she would never understand. *Maybe one day she would understand,* he thought. *I'll come back for her and my girls. That's what I'll do; I'll come back.*

John had promised to help Joy move the rest of her things to Charlene's but he hadn't arrived or even called. Joy finally got everything moved with Charlene's help and went to turn in the keys at the hotel desk. The concierge gave her a large white envelope addressed to her from John. Joy looked surprised but was praying it would explain why he did not return as promised. She opened the package and found a deed and two sets of keys to a brand new, three-bedroom home. Joy was in tears and completely ecstatic. She flipped through the pages and found another surprise. There was a cashier's check for two and a half million dollars attached to a letter from John that read,

Dearest Joy,

I've done so many things that I'm ashamed of. I've lied to you from day one. I have always been in love with you and will always be in love with you. And because of that, I have ruined your life in other ways. I can't come back to see you and the beautiful girls. I pray I could but it would cause more harm than good. Protect them, look out for them and trust no one with them. Also, whatever you do, don't come looking for me; I no longer exist as you knew me. Please accept this home and this money. I owe it to you and your children. You deserve so much more than life has handed you. I just wanted to give you the best.

Love Always,

John

Joy was in tears. "What the hell! Noooo," Joy screamed.

Charlene ran to Joy's side and asked, "What's wrong?!"

"It's John, Charlene. Something is wrong; he left this letter saying he's never coming back."

Charlene looked at the package. "Is this a real cashier's check?! Did you read it?!"

"I'm sure it is. There is also a deed to a brand new house and two sets of keys in there," Joy said sadly.

"What the hell?!" Charlene said. "Where is John?"

"I don't know but I'm about to find out. Do you think your mother will watch the girls? We need to go to Juniper!"

"Sure let's go!" said Charlene as they headed to her car and toward the interstate to find John.

Joy arrived at the little apartment complex John had taken her to only a handful of times. The apartment was empty now and Joy felt a sense of déjà vu from her experience with Dwight. She had called his cell phone several times but there was no answer. She wanted to call his office but something told her that wasn't a good idea. She pondered and pondered on how to get in contact with John outside of his business and suddenly remembered the prescription he had filled at the pharmacy the first day she met him. Joy called the pharmacy and luckily, Shay answered the phone.

"Hey Shay. This is Joy."

"Hey bigtime! How you been, baby girl?"

"Not well. But we can talk about that later. Shay, I really need a favor. I know this is against policy but can you please look through a customer's record and find an address for me?"

"Girl, you know I got you. Just don't tell anybody you got it from me. Who are we looking for?"

"I need to find out how to locate John Mack."

"Girl, you slick. So you two were kicking it after all." Shay laughed as she typed his information into the system. "Got it. His address is 222 Ellis Way Court."

Joy vaguely remembered the address now. She recalled reading it on his driver's license the very first day she met him. *But this isn't the same address as the little apartment,* she thought.

"Thanks, Shay. I'll fill you in on the drama later."

"No problem. Just make sure you remember that I didn't tell you shit!" Shay laughed and hung up the phone.

Joy and Charlene headed to the address to find an immaculate white mansion. Joy and Charlene looked at each other in awe. "What did you say this man did for a living?" Charlene asked. "I mean are you sure he wasn't dealing drugs or something? 'Cause this place looks nothing like that little apartment we just left."

"He wasn't selling drugs. He's an architect and he has his own company."

"Yeah, if you say so. Looks weird to me!"

"Stay here, Charlene. Let me see if anyone can tell me how to find him."

Joy walked up the perfectly landscaped walkway to the grand staircase that led to the oversized front double doors. She rang the doorbell and a lady answered the door. "Can I help you?" she asked.

"Yes, I'm trying to locate a Mr. John Mack. Does he happen to be here?" Joy asked.

"No ma'am, he isn't. Are you a client of his?" the lady asked.

"Ah, yes, sort of. Could you tell me where I can find him?"

"I'm sorry. I have no idea but if you like, I can take you to the study and get Mrs. Mack. She may be able to help you."

Joy felt instantly nauseous. *Did this lady just say Mrs. Mack?* As much as Joy wanted to run back to Charlene's car and scream to the hills, she wouldn't allow herself to. She needed to find out more and she needed to find out now. So she answered the lady. "Yes. Please, I would love to meet with her."

Joy was escorted through the vast estate to an elegant study. The woman turned to Joy and said, "Please have a seat and I'll go get Mrs. Conglin-Mack for you. May I have your name?"

Joy hesitated then answered, "I would rather introduce myself to her when she gets here, if that's okay?"

The woman stated, "That's fine as well." Then she hurried away to get Mrs. Mack.

Joy looked around the room. There were pictures of the ADC company in its early days on the wall. Joy now recognized the Conglin name. *This is the Conglin estate?* Joy was really curious now as to John's involvement as she looked further around the study only to find another picture; this time it was of John and a woman. As she walked closer to the picture to make out the woman, Mrs. Conglin-Mack walked into the study. Joy couldn't believe her eyes. She recognized the woman from the condominium development and now also remembered that she was the woman who helped her into the condo when she was sick with the baby.

Melinda looked at Joy with piercing eyes as she excused the hired help from their presence. "What are you doing here?" Melinda asked Joy sharply.

"I came here looking for John," Joy answered.

"You have some nerve bringing your ass to my estate looking for my husband!" Melinda spat.

"Your husband didn't inform me that he was married! I had no idea! Were you stalking me and my baby at my place? How long have you known about me?"

"Long enough to know your house breaking ass had a baby by my husband," said Melinda.

"I'm not a house breaker. Why didn't you just talk to me about John? I had no idea he was married to you. I swear!"

Melinda walked closer to Joy. "You expect me to believe that? I've seen all the pictures you have taken. I've seen you two together in restaurants and I know for a fact that your baby is my husband's bastard child! I heard you tell him at that raggedy ass restaurant!"

Joy was fuming now. "I didn't tell him nothing like that!" *Did this bitch just call my child a bastard!* Finally, it all made sense. Joy thought back to the first day she saw Melinda, when she almost lost her baby, when she helped her into the house and gave her something to drink, then left her alone. Then she thought back to when Melinda stopped in front of her daughter's stroller claiming her name was MeMe and offered to keep Sonya. Joy walked even closer toward Melinda and now they stood toe to toe and eye to eye. "Did you call my child a bastard?! My daughter is NOT a bastard!"

"I can't tell. Doesn't bas-tard define a child without a father?" Melinda spat.

"Did you try to kill my baby, you crazy bitch?! It was you, wasn't it? All along it was your ass making my life a living hell, all because you thought I was seeing your husband! You poisoned me while I was pregnant then somehow caused all my misfortune! Why the hell would you offer to keep my baby?! Why?! Were you going to hurt her too?! Where the hell is John?! I need to talk to his ass right now!"

"You don't need to say a damn thing to my husband and if you don't get your raggedy-ann ass out of my house, I will have you thrown out!"

"You're not going to do a damn thing! I'm waiting right here until John brings his ass back so we can straighten out this mess once and for all!" Joy said.

"I said get the hell out of my damn house!" Melinda yelled as she lunged at Joy and grabbed her hair. She pulled Joy's head down and began to knee her in the face. Joy screamed as blood began to pour from her nose. Joy twisted her body around but couldn't break the grip Melinda had on her hair. Joy reached toward Melinda's face and attempted to scratch at her eyes but Melinda quickly moved and landed a strong knee kick to Joy's ribcage and said, "That's called Judo, bitch! Your little poor ass wouldn't know about that, would you!" Joy collapsed to the floor as Melinda began to kick her repeatedly in the side of her head.

"I told you to get the fuck out of my house, you little whoring-ass, dirty, lying, broke bitch!" Melinda yelled as she delivered kicks to Joy's head and face between each word.

Joy lay helplessly on the floor and then she thought of her children. Suddenly, Joy caught Melinda's foot in mid-swing and snatched it from underneath her. Melinda fell backwards and hit the back of her head on the wooden fireplace mantel on the way to the floor. Joy was dizzy and bleeding but knew her life depended on her getting up from the floor before Melinda. The back of Melinda's head was bleeding but she jumped right back up like nothing had happened. Joy was up as well, but this time she lunged toward Melinda first. Joy landed on top of Melinda and started throwing blows to her face. Melinda tried to move but Joy had her completely pinned to the floor. Joy pummeled her over and over again as blood spewed from her nose and mouth. Melinda's lip was busted and eyes were blood red as Joy stated, "That's called growing up in the hood, bitch! Bet you don't know nothing about that!"

Joy suddenly felt someone grab her neck from the back of her collar and aggressively yank her from on top of Melinda. The women were fighting so hard that they didn't even see the police come in. Joy could see Charlene standing behind four other officers, looking concerned at the entire scene. A man in plainclothes pulled Melinda off the floor as well and asked, "Are you Melinda Conglin-Mack?"

Melinda wiped her bloody mouth and stated, "Yes, who the hell else's estate do you think this is!"

"Good," the man calmly stated as he looked her directly in her bloody and battered face. "I'm Detective Marc Otis and you're under arrest for the shooting of Dwight Moss. You have the right to remain silent..."

"Wait a minute! Noooo," Melinda yelled. "I didn't shoot anybody. That's a lie!"

Joy screamed, "Whatttt! That's my child's father! No, that bitch didn't shoot my child's father!"

Detective Otis cuffed Melinda and escorted her toward the door as he stated, "Your name can't save you this time, Mrs. Conglin-Mack." The detective continued to read Melinda her rights as she shouted over and over again that she did not shoot anybody.

Joy was astounded. The other officers had taken Joy into custody because of the affray. But Joy didn't care. She quickly asked the officer, "Did I hear the detective correctly? Did he say that she shot someone named Dwight Moss?"

"Yes, ma'am," the officer answered. "That's why we are here. We came to serve a warrant for her arrest and found you two in here fighting like cats and dogs. Both of you need medical attention too."

"She may need medical attention but I'm fine, Officer. I just want to know where Dwight is!" Joy stated.

The officer shook his head at the blood on both the women. "And I bet you two were fighting about this sorry ass man who isn't even here."

Joy looked at the officer and stated, "Don't judge me! Actually, it was about that crazy ass woman trying to kill my baby! But now that I've learned she also shot my child's father, she's lucky y'all are here!

"Well, you can tell all that to the detective at the precinct."

"Okay, but Officer, is Mr. Moss still alive? Can you tell me where to find him?"

"Sure, he has been in the ICU at Medview Ridge Medical Center since the night of the shooting."

"I have to go there right away," Joy stated.

"Well, the only place you're going right now is to the precinct for this assault."

Charlene walked with Joy and the officer to the patrol car. "I'll follow you there and call Patrick so we can get you out."

"Okay. Thanks Charlene," Joy said as she ducked her head and got into the patrol car to be transported away.

***

Detective Otis had been diligently working on the Dwight Moss shooting since the day of the crime. He had very few leads and he felt from day one someone was behind the lack of evidence found on the scene that night. He knew

Melinda Conglin's family had money and were capable of making a life-changing event disappear but he was lucky this time and got an anonymous tip that led him straight to the weapon used in the crime. The weapon was dusted for prints and they matched Melinda's. Now he just needed to find out why Melinda would want to shoot Dwight, and she wasn't talking. He heard Joy say Dwight was her child's father but that wouldn't explain why Melinda would shoot him. Otis decided to talk to the woman he found in the house fighting with Melinda to see if she had any information about the case.

"Hi, I'm Detective Otis. I've been investigating the shooting of a man named Dwight Moss. Do you know him?"

Joy's eyes lit up, eager to reply but she sat quiet. She knew they would come in and start asking her questions so she planned her escape. "Yes, I know Dwight Moss and I'm willing to tell you whatever you need to know, but first, I want these petty charges dropped completely."

"I don't know if I can do that," the detective said.

"Yes, you can and you will if you want me to tell you anything. All you have on me is a petty misdemeanor but she is looking at a couple of felonies. So I'm sure you can work something out, Detective Otis."

The detective knew she was right. He could easily make her charge disappear and felt any information about Dwight would strengthen his case.

"Okay. You have a deal." Detective Otis took the handcuffs off Joy's wrists. Joy took a deep breath and told the detective everything she could recall from the first time she met John. The only thing she left out was the information about the brand new house and the two and a half million dollars he left her.

Patrick and Charlene arrived at the precinct. Joy walked out gingerly, holding her side where Melinda kicked her numerous times. "Take me straight to the hospital, Patrick," Joy said.

"What's wrong with your side?"

"I'm not going there for me. I'm going there to see Dwight. He has been under our noses this whole time! I need to get there right away!"

Patrick didn't say a word as he sped toward Medview Ridge Medical Center.

Chapter 28 - Who Are You

DETECTIVE OTIS SAT at his desk and rubbed his temples. He felt a headache coming after all the information he gathered from Joy about John. He conducted an extensive check of Mr. John Mack and found some rather surprising information. The man who paraded around town for the past five years had been dead since college. Yes, Mr. John Mack was dead. He died in a car crash with three other young men after being accused of gang-raping a girl at a party late one night. The car crashed and burst into flames leaving the bodies almost unidentifiable. No one really cared what happened to the boys since they had viciously raped the girl that night. They thought it was just karma.

So who is the man impersonating John Mack now, though, and why? he thought. Detective Otis went back into the cellblock in an attempt to talk to Melinda.

"I know about your husband." Melinda sat quietly, pouting, with a big bandage wrapped around her head. "Your family had all that money but y'all couldn't figure out that the man you thought was your husband was actually dead?"

Melinda's head snapped up toward the detective. "What are you talking about?"

"John Mack. Isn't that your husband's name?"

"Yes, why?"

"Because he doesn't exist. The man has been dead for over 10 years! Do you have any idea who that man you have been married to for all these years could be?"

Melinda looked surprised and confused. "Uhhh! No! I, I had no idea.

"So, he lied to you and Joy."

"I don't know what you are talking about, Detective. My husband has been running the family company with my father for years now. He is now the CEO."

"Well, for your sake, I sure hope all the company checks require multiple signatures because the man you're talking about doesn't exist on paper. Can you tell me where he is now, Melinda?"

Melinda sat in a daze as she tried to understand everything the detective just told her about John.

My father and I were so determined to find someone to help run the company. I know he didn't let something like this slip through the cracks.

"Melinda, do you have any idea at all where John could be?"

"No, Detective, I don't. His job was his life. He told me he was adopted and that his adoptive parents were all deceased now."

"Has he ever gone by any other names, maybe a nickname or something?"

Melinda stopped to think. Then she remembered the name she found amongst John's papers months ago, *Bernard*

Bateman...hmmm, I wonder, she thought. Melinda looked up at Detective Otis and said, "Nope. He never went by anything else."

"Okay. Would you like to tell me why you shot Dwight Moss?"

"I told you, Detective, I didn't shoot Dwight Moss!"

"We have the weapon with your prints on it, Melinda. I hope you don't think your money is going to buy you out of this charge. You're facing some real time for this!"

"I'm not facing shit because I didn't do it! Where is my lawyer? I don't have anything else to say to you!"

"I know you were at the location the night of the shooting, Melinda. I have footage of your vehicle entering the area a few blocks away from where it occurred. This would be much easier for you if you tell me what happened that night. If not, I'm going to try my best to lock your rich, spoiled ass away for so long that even your mother wouldn't recognize you when you got out!"

"Is that so?" a female's voice spoke from the doorway as she entered the room.

"I don't think so, Detective. But what I do know is that you are going to take care of the paperwork to release her right away and if not, I'll have your badge, gun, house, pension and every little thing else you own."

Melinda and the Detective looked at the beautiful, well-dressed woman. She was at least twenty years older than Melinda but they had an uncanny resemblance.

"Who are you?" Detective Otis asked the woman, although he could clearly see the resemblance.

"I'm Judge Melody Conglin and the defendant's mother. You have effected an unlawful arrest. So, I suggest you release her right now before I make life a little difficult for you."

"I don't think you understand, Judge. I had a warrant for her arrest. My arrest was completely lawful."

"Yes, I know about your little arrest warrant and I reviewed it, Detective. In your affidavit in support of the arrest warrant, you listed that there were no shell casings found on the scene but the bullets that were extracted from Mr. Moss' body were a ballistics match. However, that isn't true, is it, Detective Otis? The only real fact you had on that affidavit was Melinda's prints on the gun, but there is no way the bullets matched that gun, Detective."

"What makes you believe that?" Detective Otis became nervous.

"Because the weapon you have in the evidence locker has never been fired. Release Melinda immediately, before I have you turning in your badge for a mop!"

Detective Otis knew she had him. He hadn't received the ballistics test back yet. He was so certain and anxious to close the case and felt that all the pieces pointed right to Melinda. But after learning everything about John, he now wondered if he had really done the shooting and framed Melinda for it. Also, he thought of Joy, who now believed Melinda was the shooter. Nevertheless, he knew he had to release Melinda right away. But he was going to get down to the bottom of it and then notify Joy after he determined what really went on that night.

Melinda thought the entire incident was surreal. Simply seeing her mother after all these years was wonderful. She knew she would come through for her if she really needed her, and here she was, in the flesh. Detective Moss left the cellblock to gather Melinda's release papers. Melinda turned to her mother. "Thank you, Mom; it is so nice to see you! That was perfect timing."

"Don't feed me that bullshit, Melinda. What happened to your face and why do they believe you shot that man? I had to come off my bench and fly all the way from the other side of the coast to deal with this. Even Vallario contacted me about some stuff with your husband! Where the hell is he and what the hell is going on? Tell me right now exactly what happened that night, the night of this shooting that they are accusing you of committing!

"I was so angry with John, my husband. I told you over the phone that I believed he had been seeing another woman and we had a fight, so he left. I had been drinking and I figured he was going to her house so I grabbed my gun. Just as I suspected, that's where he went. I followed him a few blocks then I pulled out my gun. The next thing I knew I heard three gunshots. I got scared and ran back to my car. I never even fired my gun. I pointed it at him and that was it. When I got back to the house he was standing in our bedroom, then I fell down the stairs, and the rest is history."

"Well, the man you saw obviously wasn't your husband, thank God. No man is worth going to jail for, child. I'm sure your father raised you better than that!"

Melinda shot her mother a harsh glance and stated, "Yes, my father did the best he could without your help!"

"Don't get sassy with me, young lady! I'm here to help you out of this mess you have gotten yourself into! So who shot the man, Melinda?"

"I have no idea! I really don't!"

"Well, what about your face? Did your husband do that to you?"

"No, Mother. His mistress came to the estate and we got in a little scuffle."

"Scuffle?! Humph, that's an understatement! Why did your father pay for all those self-defense classes when it appears you learned nothing at all!"

"You're not here to help me!" Melinda screamed. "You're here to ridicule me, as usual! You never wanted me! All you ever thought about was your other children! Why the hell are you even here now? I'm sure you're enjoying all of this!"

"Detective Otis walked back into the room in the midst of their argument to release Melinda from custody. He looked at Melody and stated, "I'm sorry for the confusion."

"Yes, you are, Detective," she retorted nastily as she and Melinda walked out the cell block and into their chauffeured vehicle. The drive was long and quiet as Melinda and her long-time estranged mother drove to the Conglin estate.

Melinda's phone rang. "Hello Wilbur. This is really a bad time."

"I know it is, Melinda. I heard from your staff what happened to you, but I really need to see you in person. I completed the investigation and you really need to sit down with me right away."

Melinda glanced over at her mother. She didn't want her to know any more than she had to, but she also knew she wasn't going anywhere anytime soon. "I'm heading to my estate. You can meet me there in about twenty minutes."

"I'll be there." Wilbur disconnected the call. He scratched the little hair that was protruding out the side of his favorite dingy old cap. *I should have told her. This is partially my fault for being so greedy. But she was such a spoiled ass in the beginning. She wasn't that bad after I got to know her. I'm going to help her fix this mess. That's all I can do now,* Wilbur thought as he walked out to meet Melinda at the estate.

Melinda and Melody walked into the estate together for the first time since Melinda was fifteen years old. The older estate staff recognized Melody and instantly greeted her with approving hugs while the younger staff wondered who the strange woman was and looked questioningly toward the two women.

They headed into the main family room and in less than five minutes, Wilbur had arrived. Wilbur extended his hand and introduced himself to Melody. Melody looked at the grungy-looking man from head to toe. She saw his hand extended but refused to shake it. Instead she said, "And who are you? This is a private matter; why are you here?"

Wilbur ignored Melody's question and turned to Melinda. "Look, I really need to talk to you in private. It's about your company."

"Private. Did you say you need to talk to her in private about the company?" Melody asked.

Wilbur looked at Melinda. He had never seen her look so battered and defeated. He couldn't believe how quiet she was as she sat half-slumped on the sofa. She was never this quiet and he knew it had something to do with this woman standing before them so he turned to the woman and stated, "Yes, that's exactly what I said."

"You apparently don't have a clue who I am. Anything you say to her you can say around me, especially if it pertains the business."

Wilbur suddenly wanted to come to Melinda's defense.

"Just because you're her attorney doesn't mean you have the right to hear everything about her life. All you need to know is about the case at hand and that's it!"

Melody began to laugh, then she turned to Melinda as she pointed to Wilbur and asked, "Who is this ignorant, grungy-looking man standing in my home?" Melinda remained quiet.

Melody turned back to Wilbur and said, "I'm afraid you really don't know who I am. Anything and everything about the business you can and will tell me because I own all this. I'm Judge Melody Scott-Conglin."

Wilbur looked at Melinda in surprise. The whole time he had stood there thinking the woman was her attorney and never paid attention to their resemblance. Melinda had never mentioned her mother and Wilbur just assumed she was dead.

Melody could see the surprise in Wilbur's face as she smirked at his nonverbal response to her statement. "That's what I thought. So like I said before, you can tell her whatever you need to tell her right now and I'm not going anywhere."

Wilbur looked toward Melinda for a slight sign of reservation but instead she discreetly nodded her head in approval.

"Where have you been?!" Wilbur forcefully asked Melody.

"Excuse me, but you don't have the right to ask me where I have been."

"Well, your daughter needed you. Were you even here for your husband's funeral? And where were you when she was in her coma?"

"You sound like you're taking all this quite personally, Mr. Grungy."

"It's Wright! Private Investigator Wilbur Wright!"

"Private investigator, huh? Yes, I see you know soooo much about my daughter and me. Your skills really precede you," Melody said sarcastically. "We have things to take care of today, so can you go ahead and state the reason for your visit?"

Wilbur turned away from Melody and faced Melinda. "This is going to be hard for you but I promise I will do everything in my power to try to help find him."

"Just spit it out, why don't you? She's out of jail; how bad can it really be? I'll have this expunged from her record and we will continue as usual!" Melody snapped.

"You're broke! The company is bankrupt! All of your accounts are below $100,000! You don't even have enough money to cover this week's payroll!"

"Whatttt!" Melody and Melinda said in unison. "That's not possible; we had over sixty million dollars in assets! What the hell are you talking about, Wilbur?" Melinda jumped off the couch now, with fire in her eyes.

"Your accountant and I went through those papers you gave me, Melinda. You know, the secret set that you had hidden from John. Well, we found a lot of discrepancies with the numbers and decided to dig a little further to find out what was going on. It turned out that your husband really was working on these business trips, but he wasn't acquiring contracts; he was selling your existing contracts."

"Whattttt!" Melody yelled. "How the hell could he do that? He didn't have controlling interest."

"Well, yes he did. In your absence and Melinda's medical condition, he was appointed the CEO. All he needed was the green light from the board of directors for any business deals. They trusted him and thought he was acquiring contracts and causing the company to grow. But instead he personally handled the business dealings and had them write the checks out to a Bernard Bateman as the accountant."

"Bernard Bateman! Who the hell is Bernard Bateman?" Melody asked.

"I believe he is Bernard Bateman. He has been Bernard Bateman all along. He just stole the identity of John Mack to get into this industry. But he is like a ghost. I have no prior records on him and this private industry doesn't require fingerprints so he has never had a fingerprint card done. Melinda, I'm sorry, but we may never find him."

Melody stood with her daughter and looked at Wilbur and said, "Oh, we will find him. He might have taken their sixty million but I still have mine! Bring me everything you have on this man. We have a huge score to settle. First, he framed my daughter for a shooting, then he steals our business and money, all after cheating on her and getting another woman pregnant. Oh yes, we will find him! Wilbur, get to work!

***

Joy and Charlene entered the hospital room. It was the first time Joy had seen Dwight in over a year. He appeared to be sleeping and looked much different than the strong handsome man he was before. His face was extremely thin, to the point that his eyes were bulging forward. His arms were thin as well, and his body looked frail under the hospital blanket. Tears fell down Joy's face as she looked toward him. She quickly ran over to his bedside to embrace him when a man that looked just like Dwight used to look walked into the hospital room. Joy stopped in her tracks before she reached the man in the bed. She wasn't sure if he was really Dwight or not. She looked back and forth at both men then asked, "Are you Dwight's brother?"

Dwayne looked at both women. Although the woman's face was battered and bruised, Dwayne could see the tears in her eyes. He immediately knew that this one must be Joy. He silently wondered what happened to her face then stated, "Yes, I'm Dwayne and you must be Joy. I have been trying to find you for my brother for some time now."

"Oh my God." She turned to Dwight, still lying in the same position. "You have a twin?!"

"He can't answer you. He hasn't awakened since the surgery." Dwayne walked past Joy to his brother. He leaned toward his motionless body and looked down.

"I have to tell you something, Joy. The last time I saw my brother was the night he told me about you. He told me about the baby and that he said some awful things to you. He was surprised you were pregnant and he didn't mean any of it. He really loved you and wanted to make things right so he left me and drove to your house that same night to apologize, but he never made it."

Joy's tears thickened. "I, I tried to find him too. I looked everywhere! The business office in Juniper was closed and the other one was a Post Office box. I never met you or his family, and the lounge where I met him wouldn't give me any information. I even tried to file a missing person report, but they wouldn't let me. It never dawned on me that he was right here in my own town in the hospital." Tears poured from Joy's eyes. "I tried to find him, I swear I did! I thought he didn't want our baby and abandoned me! What was I to think?"

Dwayne sat his coffee cup down and reached out to hug Joy. "He loved you. He really did." Dwayne released Joy then pulled out the little black box that he had carried around for his brother for this very moment. "My brother wanted to apologize to you and give you this the night he was shot." Dwayne opened the box to reveal the beautiful ring Dwight had bought for her. "He was going to ask you to marry him." Joy's tears were full stream now as she looked over at Dwight lying in the hospital bed. "Take it, Joy. He wanted you to have it." Dwayne took the beautiful three-carat ring out of its velvet case and handed it to Joy. "Do with it as you like. It belongs to you." Joy walked over and stood beside Dwight and placed the ring on her finger. She leaned to his ear and said, "Yes. Yes, Dwight Moss, I will marry you. Now you wake up. Come back to us. Your daughter and I will be waiting." She placed a kiss on the side of his face and sat in the chair beside his bed for hours, waiting for the doctor. She was determined to find a way to help Dwight, and she had two and a half million dollars to do it.

Joy and Dwayne talked about John and what happened the whole day up to this moment. Dwayne was furious and wanted to find Melinda and John. "They will pay for what happened to my brother," Dwayne said angrily.

"I have to leave now, Dwayne. I just moved to Newcomb and my children are there with my aunt."

They exchanged information and Dwayne vowed to introduce her and Sonya to his family. They hugged and Joy left. Joy and Charlene arrived back in Newcomb, only to find that Timothy had driven there and picked up the children from Ruth's.

Joy immediately dialed Timothy's cell phone. "Timothy! Why do you have my children?" Joy screamed in the phone.

"Whoa, whoa, slow your role, woman. I was just trying to help. Your brother called me about maybe getting Sophie for a few days. Sounds like you had some major drama going on. Sophie wanted her sister to come along too, so I took both of them. What's the problem? You know I would never hurt the girls."

"I'm sorry, Timothy. There has been a lot going on today, between John, Melinda and even Dwight."

"Dwight? What about Dwight?" Timothy asked.

"He has been in the hospital all this time. Right there in Medview Ridge Medical Center in Juniper!

"Sonya's father?! Really?! Hmmmm," Timothy said.

"Yeah, I met his brother and everything. This has just been too much for one day. Not to mention that our newfound friendship is still awkward to me. I need time to adjust. Can you just bring the girls back home? I'm staying at Charlene's for a few days."

"Sure, baby. I'll meet you there right now."

"Timothy, please don't call me baby. We are divorced and I don't want the children confused."

"Okay, okay, I feel ya. I'll see you in a few." Timothy disconnected the call, gathered the children and their things and put them in the car. He wasn't far from Newcomb and thought of Joy and her situation as he got closer to Charlene's place. *Man, dude. What am I going to do now? That weak motherfucker better not wake up. Fucking with my wife! She will always be my wife, divorced or not. I'm slowly working my way back into her heart now. I can tell it! She might not know it but I do. Patrick and Susan even trust me again. Yeah, I got this one under wraps! I just thought that motherfucker was dead. I shot his punk ass three times! Well, since I see now that he isn't dead, I might have to go to that hospital and finish his ass off once and for all!*

Twisted Deception II

Leticia Twyman

Through the darkness, she could feel his presence looking directly at her. He reached over and pulled her body closer, until her chin touched his bare chest. She could feel his heart beating and feel his breath upon her skin. The room was silent as he reached down and tenderly touched her face, slowly lifting it to meet his gaze that was only illuminated by the dim light coming from the clock on the headboard. As he gazed into her eyes he softly stated, "I love you. I love everything about you." She shivered at his touch as his lips softly touched hers. They passionately kissed as they always had. They passionately embraced like they always would. And at that moment everything that seemed so wrong, so terrible, so painful, all disappeared and they were back as they were once before in each other's arms and in inseparable love with each other...

Email this author at:

Leticia.twyman@yahoo.com

www.lbtproducts.com

ABOUT THE AUTHOR

Leticia Twyman was born in South Carolina but raised in the Washington, DC area. She's a multi-talented artist and entrepremeur who strives to deliver a quality product to her readers each and every time. The married mother of three and proud grandmother of four, loves to connect with her readers via email or blog posts for book content ideas, input and motivational direction for future projects. Look forward to many more titles from this author in the future starting with Twisted Deception Part Two on EBook and paperback.

Email this author at:
leticia.twyman@yahoo.com

www.ingramcontent.com/pod-product-compliance
Lightning Source LLC
Chambersburg PA
CBHW072055170626
46813CB00004B/1365
* 9 7 8 0 9 9 7 4 0 3 3 1 2 *